Captain Calliope and the Great Goateenies

A Bailey Fish Adventure

Linda Salisbury

Drawings by Carol Tornatore

Tabby House

Cover design and illustrations: Carol Tornatore
Author photo: Elaine Taylor

Library of Congress Control Number: 2009933216

ISBN-13: 978-1-881539-48-3

ISBN-10: 1-881539-48-2

Manufactured within CPSIA guidelines.
United Graphics, Inc.
Mattoon Il 61938 USA
10/10/2009

Batch #1

Classroom quantities and *Teacher's Guides*
available by contacting the publisher.

baileyfish@gmail.com
www.BaileyFishAdventures.com
www.BaileyFishAdventureBooks.blogspot/com

Tabby House
P.O. Box 544, Mineral, VA 23117

(540) 895-9093

Contents

1

Mysterious Truck

The air was steamy hot when Bailey Fish rolled out of bed and stretched. Her snoring hound dog, Goldie, and young cats, Shadow and Sallie, didn't stir. Shadow rolled on his back on Bailey's pillow, and Sallie's ears twitched, but they were still asleep.

The big green T-shirt Bailey slept in was damp from sweat. Her upstairs bedroom in her grandmother's house was often hot, even with the fan humming on her desk. Bailey wondered if the Virginia weather would cool down before middle school started in a few weeks. The sticky heat reminded her of Florida where she used to live.

Bailey glanced at her alarm clock. She would have time to read a few more chapters in one of her favorite books, *Charlotte's Web*, before breakfast. Her mother read it with her five years earlier when she was six. Two days ago, Bailey found a very old copy in her grandmother's library. Sugar said it was quite valuable, but wanted Bailey to enjoy reading it. "Just be careful."

Bailey curled up in the green and yellow overstuffed chair in her cozy dormer window. It was her favorite place in Sugar's house. The red café curtains with white stars trembled in the slight morning breeze, and leaves from a large tulip poplar tree brushed the window. They seemed to call Bailey to hurry outside.

Bailey picked up her book and carefully opened the brittle yellow pages to chapter 7, titled "Bad News." She had just reached the part in which the sheep informed Wilbur, the pig, what the bad news was, when she gazed out the window. Bailey thought she saw someone at the end of the driveway. It was her grandmother.

She leaned over and peered out of her window through the thick branches of the tree. Cobwebs the size of dinner plates dotted the lawn. They were filled with morning dew and sparkled in the sunlight. Bailey watched Sugar pull the newspaper from its white plastic tube, then look west down the narrow country road. Sugar seemed to be studying something headed in her direction.

Bailey ran her fingers through her light-brown hair. She was about to read more when she saw a small, colorfully decorated truck pull up and stop at the end of the driveway. Bailey squinted, but couldn't read the words on the white truck's side. It looked as if there were pictures of fanciful animals, like unicorns, on it. They seemed to be leaping through hoops and balancing on large balls.

Sugar pointed in the direction of Keswick Inn, where Bailey's friends, Noah and Fred Keswick, and their foster sister, Sparrow, lived.

Bailey carefully placed *Charlotte's Web* on a small table next to her writer's notebook and a new postcard of the rain forest from her mother. Then she quickly changed into her denim shorts and a T-shirt and slipped into her old sandals with straps. She looked out the window again. The truck was gone, and Sugar was reading the newspaper headlines as she walked back up the driveway.

Goldie and the cats were now awake and waiting for her near the bedroom door. Bailey smoothed her sheets and antique quilt, and rushed downstairs.

She reached the kitchen at the same time as her grandmother.

"Who was that?" Bailey asked. She hunted for her blue cereal bowl in the sink drainer.

"A former circus guy," said Sugar. "He's looking for a place to stay for a few days. He'd heard about Keswick Inn and hopes they'll let him keep his animals there."

"Animals? What kind of animals?" Bailey asked. This sounded like an adventure. She reached for the oat cereal box in the pantry cupboard.

"I'm not exactly sure," said Sugar. She took a long sip of coffee. "From the pictures on the truck, I'd say the animals do tricks. Guess we'll have to go to the Keswicks' to see."

"I'll be ready in a minute," said Bailey. She pushed away her bowl of half-eaten cereal.

"Not so fast," said Sugar, "I think you and *your* animals need breakfast first."

Bailey hurriedly finished her crunchy cereal, then scooped kibble into bowls for her pets. Goldie gulped her food. Bailey knew her Walker hound was still trying to make up for all the time she lived alone in the woods after being abandoned. Goldie still seemed afraid that she wouldn't get enough to eat.

"It's okay, girl," said Bailey. "You can have more later."

Goldie licked her bowl, slurped from her large orange water dish, and picked up her leash.

"You can go with us," said Bailey.

Sugar opened the screen door and said, "Sure is hot at this hour. I'll be glad when we have a hint of fall. At least cooler nights and mornings. It won't be long now."

It'll be Christmas time before it's chilly in Florida, Bailey thought. *I wonder if Mom and I will be home by then. Probably not. She likes Costa Rica and Bug Man too much.*

Before her throat could swell with a lump of sadness, Bailey grabbed Goldie's leash.

The dog knew the path through the woods to the Keswicks' house. Sugar and Bailey followed her across the yard.

"There's the truck!" exclaimed Bailey when they reached the field behind the inn.

The box-shaped white truck with brightly colored circus letters and animal designs was parked near the big barn. Bailey could see Mr. Will and Miss Bekka, Noah and Fred's parents, talking with a short, bald man. He had sideburns that looked like squirrels' tails. They reached from in front of his ears to his chin. The man's hand was on the back door of the truck. He lifted the latch.

"Hurry, Sugar!" said Bailey. She wanted to be there when the door opened so she could see what was inside.

"Run on ahead," said her grandmother. "I'll be right along."

Bailey and Goldie dashed across the field and through the apple orchard to the barn.

2

Goateenies Arrive

Bailey reached the truck about the same time as Noah and Fred came running from the house. They looked as if they had thrown on their clothes. The boys had apparently been in as much of a rush as Bailey, who had just realized that she hadn't bothered to brush her hair.

Noah's unruly hair, the color of a yellow cat's, was sticking out funny on one side and was flat on the other, where he'd been sleeping on it. Fred had covered his dark curly hair with one of his many baseball caps. He hadn't noticed that his shirt was on backwards.

"I don't see any problem with the animals staying here," Mr. Will said to the man. "It won't take long for us to make a pen in the barn. You'll have to take care of their food, though. I don't have any tasty tin cans." Mr. Will grinned.

Animals? Tin cans? What was Mr. Will talking about? Bailey couldn't wait for the man to open the truck. She held Goldie's leash close to her collar.

"Now," said the man, with a deep bow, "I present the amazing, stupendous, outstanding, fantastical, magical Great Goateenies." With that he opened the latch.

Bleh.

A whiskery face looked out.

It was a small black and white goat. "This is Gruff," announced the man. "My No. 1 Goateenie."

Bleh, bleated Gruff. He hopped out of the truck. The man hooked a rope leash on Gruff's wide gold collar and handed it to Fred.

"Are there more Goateenies inside?" asked Bailey. Her hazel eyes opened wide.

"Yes, and no," said the man. "Who are you?"

"I'm Bailey, and this is Sugar. We're—"

The man interrupted. "Pleased to meet you. I'm Captain Calliope—that's pronounced '*Cal-ee-yoap*.' I'm owner and trainer of the famed Great Goateenies. These are the new ones, though. There used to be others in the act—little Ruben, and Finch, their sister, Bella—and my assistant, the beautiful, talented Zola Mira. We had a terrible misunderstanding.

Terrible. And they went away many towns back. Now I'm left with just Gruff. It's hard to do the act with just one Goateenie. What's worse, he was new to the show and never learned the tricks."

"What kind of act?" asked Noah.

"The real Great Goateenies are very clever," said Captain Calliope. "I trained them to jump through hoops, kick balls, dance ballet, and do the pyramid. I have pictures. I'll show you."

There was a loud thumping inside.

"What's that?" asked Fred. Gruff was nibbling the sweet grass by his feet.

"That's Bunny," said Captain Calliope.

Bunny? It must be a really huge rabbit to make that loud noise, thought Bailey.

"Bunny's a potbellied pig. She used to be a racing pig at county fairs. Always came in third, the last of three." Captain Calliope twisted the ends of his sideburns.

"I also have my rooster, Caruso. He's never been trained before. The pig and rooster are both new to my show, and I need a few weeks to train them to work with Gruff. I may call the act 'The New Great Goateenies.'" He opened his arms wide with the announcement. "I hope the traveling show takes me back."

Captain Calliope motioned to Mr. Will to assist him. They unlatched the hinges of a wooden crate. Bunny snuffled and yawned.

The two men lifted the fat pig with short legs to the ground. She rolled happily in the grass. Next came Caruso, a handsome creature with brightly colored shiny feathers—red, orange, yellow, and black. Caruso cocked his head, spotted a bug in the grass, and snatched it with his yellow beak.

"Do you need separate pens for Bunny and Gruff today?" asked Mr. Will. Bailey could tell he wanted to laugh out loud from the way his green eyes sparkled. "It will take a couple of days to fix up the barn for them."

"No, they can bunk together overnight," said Captain Calliope.

"Caruso can stay in the back side of the Chicken Coop Theater," offered Fred. "We're going to put chickens in there someday—when we save enough money to buy them."

"Fine. Splendid. Magnificent," said Captain Calliope. He surveyed the barn and yard. "This is the perfect spot for me to put together my new act." He looked around at Bailey, Fred, Noah, and Sparrow, who had just arrived in her wheelchair. "And you, my friends, will help me do it!"

3

Settling In

"Boys, see if Captain Calliope needs help carrying his things to his room. He'll be in room five. I'm going to call Justin to see if he can help me pound pens together," said Mr. Will.

"Okay, Dad," said Noah. He walked over to the truck with Fred. The captain handed him a large brown suitcase and tossed a cardboard box to Fred. The box was labeled PROGRAMS AND CLIPPINGS.

Sugar told Miss Bekka she'd make lemonade for everyone, and the two women went into the house.

Within minutes, Justin Rudd, a quiet neighborhood boy, rode over on his bike. He was followed by Ninja, his scruffy brown mutt. Justin dropped his bike and walked quickly to the truck.

Bailey could tell Justin was impressed by the paintings on the truck and the animals.

He studied the elegant letters and knelt down to pet Bunny and Gruff. Caruso was wary of the newcomer. He cocked his head and stepped away.

Bailey thought, *Justin will like having the act here. He's so good at training animals.* Justin was able to teach the boys' naughty dog, Clover, to mind him, and he had even trained the pet crow that he had rescued and raised.

"We're all going to help with the act," Bailey told Justin. He nodded and smiled—something Bailey rarely saw him do.

"The *real* Goateenies," Justin said softly, as if he had heard of them. He patted Gruff one more time and went into the barn to find Mr. Will.

Fred had tied Gruff's leash to Sparrow's wheelchair while he helped carry two brown paper sacks into the inn. Then the captain asked the boys to place a large trunk, several hoops, folding platforms, stools, and a unicycle just inside the barn.

"Props for the Goateenies," he said. "What an act this will be! Too bad Ruben, Finch, Bella, and Zola Mira aren't here."

"Are you from the circus?" asked Sparrow.

"My young friend, I've been in big tops large and small. I've traveled the world. I've been to big cities. I decided to go out on my own. Then, I became a carney—taking my Goateenies to small carnivals and county fairs and recently, a small family circus."

"I went on carnival rides once," said Sparrow, "before I had to sit in this stupid chair. I really liked the Ferris wheel and the rollercoaster. We ate blue cotton candy and fried baloney sandwiches."

Captain Calliope smiled kindly. "It's the roving life for me," he said. "Now, if you'll keep an eye on Gruff, I'll get out the food for the animals. Bunny won't go far on those little legs of hers, but Gruff likes to explore and climb."

Just then, Gruff put his dainty front feet on the arms of Sparrow's wheelchair and stuck his whiskery beard in her face.

"He's got weird eyes, but he likes me," said Sparrow, giggling. She touched his nubby horns.

"Here, give him this," said the captain, handing her a carrot. "He won't bite you if you hold it on a flat palm."

Bailey smiled and watched Gruff nibble the carrot out of the seven-year-old's hand.

4

Circus Planning

"Dudes, I've been thinking," said Noah. "As long as Captain Calliope and the Goateenies are staying with us, why don't we have a circus of our own? We could come up with other acts, charge admission, and raise money for something, like buying our chickens."

"Awesome idea," said Bailey.

"I want to be the bareback rider," said Sparrow.

When nobody responded she added, "It doesn't matter if I'm in a wheelchair because we don't have real horses anyway. It's just pretend, you know."

"Okay," said Fred. He wrote her name and "bareback rider" next to it on a lined yellow pad. "Who's going to be the ringmaster?"

Bailey thought he sounded as if he wanted someone to say his name. Instead, Noah quickly volunteered, "I will."

"But I'd like to do it," said Fred.

"We'll flip a coin," said Noah. "Heads you win." He tossed a quarter in the air and it landed heads up. "Okay, bro," said Noah. "I'll be the lion trainer."

"We don't have a lion," said Sparrow.

"We have Clover and Goldie," said Noah. "They'll do just fine."

Bailey tried to think of something she could do for the show. She remembered the circus that she and her mother, Molly, had attended in Florida a few months before her mother went to Costa Rica for her "dream job." Her mother won a lucky ticket that allowed her to ride on an elephant during the circus parade. Bailey and her best friend, Amber, yelled and screamed when the parade, led by a clown on stilts, entered the big top. Then, there was Molly, hanging on tightly to the spangling harness of Helen, the elephant.

Molly waved and blew kisses when she passed the bleacher seats where Bailey and Amber were shouting her name. Bailey held up Molly's camera, but she was so excited that her hands jiggled. The picture of Molly riding on Helen was crooked and fuzzy. Molly laughed when she saw it and said, "That's the way I felt up there. Crooked and fuzzy."

From high in the bleachers, they watched dancing ponies, a white tiger act, trapeze artists in glittery aqua costumes, clown jugglers, acrobats, and the Human Cannonball. He was shot out of a cannon and landed in a big net way across the tent. Bailey and Amber screamed and covered their ears when the cannon boomed.

Bailey watched a girl about her age who wore a silver suit. The girl bowed and stood on the end of a balance board. Another acrobat jumped on the other end, and the girl flew through the air, did three somersaults, and landed gracefully on her feet. *I bet it would be fun to be in the circus,* Bailey thought.

After the show was over, they walked outside into the cool night air, trying to remember where Molly had parked her car. Bailey saw the girl in the silver suit selling popcorn. The circus already was being packed up. Molly said it would all be gone in the middle of the night, and by dawn the big top would be raised in another city. Bleachers would be unfolded. The performers would be ready for two more shows the next day and the next.

"Look, there's my Helen!" exclaimed Molly. The large gray elephant was pulling a little train of tiger cages.

"Hi, Helen. Remember me, girl? I know elephants don't forget," Molly said, making Bailey laugh.

"That ride was an adventure. I love adventure," Molly said, hugging Bailey and Amber.

Then, just a few months later Molly left on her own new-job adventure and sent Bailey to live in Virginia with her grandmother.

"Bailey. Bailey! Daydreaming again?" asked Noah. "You haven't said what you want to be in the circus."

Bailey blushed when she realized that everyone was looking at her. "I don't know," she said. "Maybe I could be an acrobat and sell popcorn."

"Deal," said Fred. He wrote it down on his yellow pad.

5

Bunny's Duck

When Bailey arrived at Keswick Inn the next morning, Captain Calliope was sitting on a bale of hay with his head in his hands. He didn't seem to notice her walking through the orchard with Goldie. Bailey saw him shake his head and heard him sigh deeply.

"Hi," said Bailey.

The man looked up quickly, smoothed his fuzzy sideburns, and smiled. "Would you like to feed the Goateenies?" he asked.

"Sure," said Bailey. "What should I do?"

He handed her a small pan of grain and two apples for Gruff and Bunny. He said he had corn for Caruso. The rooster was crowing in the back part of the old, fixed-up chicken coop. "Don't overfeed them, and only give them healthy food," the captain said.

Just as Bailey went into the barn with the food, the boys rushed out from the house.

"Hey, we want to help," said Noah. He took the apples and walked ahead of Bailey to where the animals were penned.

"I brought carrots," said Fred, "and lettuce. I don't think Mom'll mind."

Captain Calliope followed them inside. "After the Goateenies have breakfast and Bunny has a bath, we'll talk about their act."

"How do you train them?" asked Bailey. "I mean, isn't that hard?"

"Very," said Captain Calliope. "And it takes time. I won't be able to rejoin the Otto Brothers Traveling Show anytime soon."

"Otto Brothers?" said Noah.

"They aren't a large show. They play a lot of small towns, like the early American circuses did. Now, my friends, down to business." The captain pointed to Fred. "You, young man, may give Bunny her bath. She loves to have her back scrubbed. And I have her rubber duck somewhere in my truck."

"Bunny has a rubber duck?" asked Fred.

"I've been trying to teach her to balance it on her nose," said Captain Calliope. "So far, all she wants to do is eat it. Don't let her."

"I'll be careful," said Fred.

"What sort of act will the Goateenies do?" asked Noah.

"My plan is to have Gruff jump through hoops, tap his front hoof ten times when I tell him to, then climb on Bunny's back while she balances the duck on her nose. Meanwhile, Caruso will fly up and land on top of Gruff's horns. It will be magnificent. The crowds will go wild for the New Great Goateenies."

Bailey tried to imagine how this act would look in the center ring with spotlights shining on the captain and his animals.

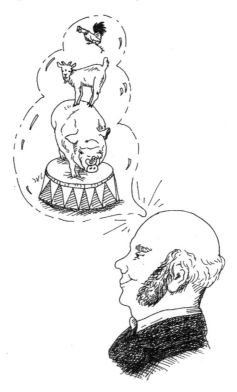

"How will you get them to do that?" asked Noah. "Won't the goat get scared when the rooster dude lands on his head? I would." He crossed his arms over his chest.

Captain Calliope said, "That's my problem. I've never worked with this combo before, just the original Goateenies. But, my dear friends, with your help, the new act will take shape. We can do it. Yes, we can." He twisted his sideburns. They sprung back when he let go.

He sounds like he's trying to convince himself, Bailey thought. *And he doesn't look convinced.*

The captain sighed deeply and walked back to his truck.

Fred led Bunny out of the dark barn into the sunny yard. She trotted with him to where a green garden hose was coiled. Fred looked at Captain Calliope for further instructions, but the man just nodded for Fred to continue. So Fred turned on the water and sprayed the pig. Bunny tried to catch the stream of water in her mouth. She shook and rolled vigorously. Fred looked again at Captain Calliope. The man smiled, nodded, and pointed to a large scrub brush.

Fred put the hose down, picked up the soft brush, and gently rubbed Bunny's belly and then her back when she stood up. She snuffled and drooled happily.

"There," said Fred. He was soaking wet.

"Now, see if you can make her balance the rubber duck." Captain Calliope tossed the yellow toy to Fred. Fred looked at the man and then at the pig. He pushed his round glasses up his nose, then squatted in front of the pig.

"Sit, Bunny," said Fred. The pig stared at him, then pulled toward the barn.

"I mean it. Sit!" said Fred. He tried to get her attention by squeaking the duck. Bunny ignored him.

"Some ringmaster you make," said Noah. He had Gruff on a leash by his side. The goat wanted to nibble Miss Bekka's red, pink, and yellow zinnias.

"Sit, Bunny," Fred pleaded. He squeaked the duck again.

Bunny had other plans. She tugged on her rope until Fred had to follow her toward Miss Bekka's vegetable garden. Fred stopped her just short of the rows of yellow squash.

"No, you don't. Mom'll be mad," said Fred. Bunny continued to pull toward the garden.

This isn't working, thought Bailey. *Now what?*

6

The Captain's Errands

"My friends, I'm leaving you in charge for a while," said Captain Calliope the next morning. "I worked with the Goateenies until late and have decided to go to town to get extra supplies. Sweet-smelling straw for their beds and savory corn and other Goateenie treats. I also have pressing errands. Do you think you can handle things while I'm gone?" His fingers stroked his sideburns as if they were alive.

"Sure," said Bailey. The boys shook their heads in agreement.

"Don't let them wander," the captain said. "No junk food."

"We're on top of it," said Noah.

"Should we let Caruso out?" asked Fred.

"Good idea," said the captain. "The old bird might like to stretch his wings and scratch for grubs, but keep an eye on him. He's new to the act, you know. He hasn't bonded yet with

Bunny or Gruff. This trio is not like my other Goateenies. They were really close. Worked well together. Never a problem." He turned his head away and blew his nose in a large red handkerchief.

Bailey wanted to ask why the other Goateenies and Zola Mira were gone, but Captain Calliope sounded so unhappy she didn't dare. He cleared his throat, put his hankie in his pants pocket, and smiled.

Captain Calliope then scratched Bunny's ears, petted Gruff between the horns, and nodded in the direction of the chicken coop where Caruso was perched in the window.

"The show must go on. Take care of them," he said. "I'm counting on you."

"We will. We like animals," Bailey said.

Captain Calliope climbed into his truck and drove off.

"Well, dudes, what should we do first?" asked Noah.

"Eat," said Fred. "I didn't have breakfast."

"How can you think about food at a time like this?" asked Noah. "We're in charge of the new Great Goateenies, and maybe we can get them trained before the captain comes back."

"I train better with food," said Fred, and he jogged to the house.

"Then make sandwiches for all of us, bro," shouted Noah.

Bailey wasn't sure Fred had heard Noah's request, but she hoped so because her stomach was growling.

She held the pan of grain out for Gruff and thought about how life had become one huge adventure since she had arrived at Sugar's house during the winter.

Bailey heard Sparrow calling, "Fred, wait up. Wait for me. I'll help you."

7

First Trick

Fred *had* heard Noah. His sandwiches were thick with bologna and Swiss cheese. Sparrow wheeled right behind him. She carried a large, wrinkled brown paper bag.

"I brought extra apples and bananas. Some for us and some for the Goateenies," she said.

"I thought you were helping Mom bake bread today," said Noah.

"I was, but she got a phone call and went in her bedroom and closed the door so I couldn't hear what she was saying," said Sparrow. She pushed her long bangs out of her face.

Gruff trotted over to her and put his feet on the arms of the wheelchair. "I think he wants an apple," said Sparrow.

"Don't reward him unless he does a trick," said Bailey. "Let's see if we can get him to stand on Bunny's back. We'll surprise Captain Calliope."

31

Bunny dozed under the apple tree. Fred tugged on her rope, but she wouldn't budge.

"She looks like a speed bump," said Noah. "Wake up, piggy," he said.

"I can't move her," said Fred. He tugged again, but the pig only grunted.

"Then, let's take Gruff to her," said Bailey.

Sparrow held an apple in the air and wheeled close to Bunny. Gruff pranced beside her, trying to steal the fruit from her hand.

"Hold it above Bunny," said Noah. Sparrow reached as high as she could. But, instead of standing on the pig, Gruff jumped over Bunny.

"Hey, that's great. That's a trick. Make her do it again," said Fred.

Sparrow tossed the apple to Noah, who was standing on the other side of the pig, and Gruff sailed over. Noah tossed the apple to Fred, and back went Gruff. Bunny didn't seem to care. After the fifth time, Fred said, "Give Gruff the apple as a reward. Boy, won't the captain be surprised! It's almost as good as—maybe better than—jumping through a hoop."

"Where's Captain Calliope?" asked Sparrow.

"Town," said Bailey.

"Oh," said the little girl.

"This act'll be great in our show," said Noah.

"If Captain Calliope lets us," said Bailey.

8

Worries

Bailey heard the screen door *whap* shut and saw Miss Bekka hurrying to the barn where Mr. Will was repairing the rung of a kitchen chair. She looked worried.

After a few minutes they came out of the barn together and headed for the house. Mr. Will had his arm around her shoulder.

Sparrow was watching them, too. "Maybe it was the phone call," she said. "I hope it's not about me."

"Why would they be upset about you?" asked Bailey.

Sparrow didn't answer. She glanced at the house, started to wheel toward it, then stopped, as if an invisible hand was holding her back.

A few minutes later Bailey was surprised to see Sugar drive up. She parked her red pickup truck near the back door. She waved to Bailey and her friends and went inside.

What's going on? wondered Bailey. Sugar hadn't said anything about visiting Miss Bekka this morning. The boys didn't seem to be aware of anything other than the Goateenies.

"One more time, Gruff," said Fred, who was still working on tricks. "Jump!" Gruff looked at the apple in his hand, and jumped. At that moment, Bunny decided to stand up. It surprised the goat. Instead of sailing over the pig, Gruff landed on Bunny's back. He only perched there for a second because Bunny squealed and tried to get away.

"We did it! We did it!" said Noah and he gave Fred a high-five.

Bailey grinned, but stopped when she saw Sparrow cover her face with her hands.

9

Bad News

Sugar was the first adult to come out of the house. She bent forward as if she were carrying a heavy backpack. When she reached Bailey, she said, "I meant to tell you that Emily's home from camping and wants you to call her. I told her you were here, so she might show up later."

Emily and her family had been camping for almost a month in the Shenandoah Valley. She had sent Bailey two postcards—one of the stalactite organ deep within Luray Cavern, and one of a view of the mountains near where they camped by the river.

Without waiting for Bailey to answer, Sugar leaned down and gave Sparrow a hug. "Miss Bekka and Mr. Will want to talk with you, sweetheart."

"I knew it," said Sparrow. She sounded afraid. Without looking at the other kids, she slowly rolled her chair toward the house, tightly gripping the wheels.

Noah and Fred stopped tossing the apple. "What's going on?" asked Fred. He walked after her.

"Wait," Sugar said. "I'll fill you in."

When Sparrow was out of earshot, Sugar said, "As you probably know, Miss Bekka and Mr. Will have been talking about adopting Sparrow. She's been in foster homes almost all her life, but before she can be adopted, her birth family must sign papers. Will and Bekka thought this was going to happen easily, but this morning Miss Bekka had a call from Sparrow's caseworker. "

"What's a caseworker?" asked Bailey. She twisted her hair and pushed it behind her ear.

"The caseworker is the person who knows all about Sparrow and finds good foster homes for her," said Sugar.

Noah and Fred walked closer to listen.

"They aren't going to take Sparrow away from us?" said Fred. His voice cracked.

"Just let them try!" said Noah. "She's our little sister now." He put his hands on his hips.

Bailey's eyes stung.

"There's a problem," said Sugar. "Sparrow apparently has a birth aunt she's never met who says that she might want to adopt Sparrow. It's all very complicated."

"No!" shouted Fred. He yanked off his baseball cap and threw it at the barn.

"Nothing's definite," said Sugar. "There'll be a visit. We all want her to stay, but—"

"When's the old witch coming?" asked Noah.

Instead of telling Noah not to say bad things about Sparrow's aunt, Sugar put her arm around him.

"This is hard for all of us. Sparrow knows she's loved here and she'll never forget that, no matter what happens. All we can do is hope for the best for her."

"When's the visit?" repeated Noah. He kicked at a clump of dirt.

"Probably within the next two weeks," said Sugar. "Now, your folks have just one request of all of you. Try to keep from being upset around Sparrow. We all need to make things as normal as possible for her. She'll be worried enough."

"Oh, sure. We find out that we might lose our Sparrow, and we're supposed to pretend that everything's okay," said Fred. He looked at Sugar's face and quickly apologized. "I'm sorry, Sugar. We'll try."

10

Naughty Goateenies

"Hey, guys, I'm back!" shouted Emily. No one had noticed that her mother had dropped her off in the driveway.

"What's the matter? Isn't anyone going to say hi?" Emily tossed her dark curly hair and put her hands in her pockets. "And what are those animals doing here?"

Bailey tried to push Sparrow from her mind. She gave her friend a hug. "Hi, Em. Missed you," she said.

"Missed you, too. I brought presents for everyone, but they're not unpacked yet," said Emily. "And look at my tan. I laid out every day." She held out her arms to show them. "Now will you tell me what those goofy animals are doing here?"

Bailey turned to where Bunny and Gruff had been lounging near the apple tree. While no one was watching, their ropes had come loose. Gruff had climbed on the hood of Mr. Will's truck, and Bunny had finally reached Miss Bekka's garden and was munching on squash.

"Oh, no!" said Noah. The boys ran to capture the wanderers.

"Come back, Bunny!" said Noah. "Mom's going to be really mad. That's her special garden." He grabbed at the pig's rope.

"So, did the Keswicks get new pets?" asked Emily.

Fred was trying to talk Gruff down from the truck. The goat's short rope leash was just out of reach. In fact, Gruff was sizing up the roof of the cab. With a quick hop, he was on the very top. *Bleh. Bleh.*

Sugar laughed out loud. "No they are just visiting Keswick Inn."

Bailey said, "Gruff, the goat, Bunny, the pig, and Caruso, the rooster, all belong to

Captain Calliope. They are the New Great Goateenies. Captain Calliope is teaching them a new act. While they're here, we're going to have a circus of our own to raise money."

"Good. I want to be in it. I'll be the beautiful trapeze artist," said Emily. "Why do you call him Captain "*Cal*-ee-yoap? I thought it is pronounced "Cal-*eye*-o-pee?"

"It's the way circus people say the word," said Sugar. "Captain Calliope prefers the circus pronunciation, but it is hard for the rest of us to always remember. By the way, where *is* the captain?"

"He went to town and left us in charge of the Goateenies," said Bailey.

"When did he say he'd be back?" asked her grandmother.

Bailey thought back to his words. "I don't know. He didn't say." Suddenly she felt uneasy. "He sort of said good-bye. It was weird. He was sad."

"I doubt that it was really good-bye," said Sugar. "He loves these animals and has big plans for his new act." She looked at her watch. "My goodness, I'd better get back home. First, I'll give Fred a hand."

Fred was still trying to coax Gruff down. Sugar opened the truck's door, stood on the running board, reached up, and grabbed the rope.

"Now, Fred, get some old blankets from the barn, and put them on the hood so that when he jumps, he won't make a dent."

"Why didn't I think of that?" muttered Fred.

With the blankets protecting the hood, Sugar tugged on the rope and said, "Easy does it, boy."

Bleh. Gruff tossed his head, eyed the thick blankets, and jumped down, first on the hood, then to the ground.

"You're going into your pen, you bad kid," said Fred. He reached the barn at the same time that Noah appeared dragging Bunny. The pig was still chomping on squash.

11

Emily Plans a Party

"Bailey, Mom says I can have a slumber party—a makeup party—before school starts. I learned a lot about makeup and hair this summer from Valerie, a girl where we camped," Emily told Bailey. "And I told her all about you—how you never wear makeup or dress up. Valerie said I should help you."

"I might be busy," said Bailey. She wanted to follow the boys back to the animals' pens instead of talking about makeup.

"Busy? But I want you to come. I know just the right lip gloss for you," said Emily, with a smile that Bailey didn't like. "Just like mine."

Bailey's face reddened. She had noticed that Emily looked different than before she went away for vacation. Her lips were shiny, and she seemed to have pinker cheeks.

"I really don't like makeup," Bailey said. She turned away.

"I bet you've never tried it, Bails," said Emily. "Besides, boys will like you better."

"They like me fine," said Bailey. She watched Noah and Fred wash their hands with soap and a hose after shutting the Goateenies in their pens. The adopted twelve-year-olds were her friends. Best friends. That's the way Bailey wanted things to be.

"Don't you want to go out?" asked Emily.

"I'm just eleven," said Bailey. She wished Emily would talk about something else.

"We start middle school soon," said Emily. "My parents won't let me go out, either, but I want boys to ask me on a date, anyway."

Bailey wasn't sure what to say. She was glad when Noah and Fred joined them.

"There, the Goateenies are safe and sound. The captain will never know that they got loose," said Noah.

"So, we're going to have a circus," said Emily. Her dimples showed when she smiled.

"That's the plan," said Fred. "We need to start working on it so that the Goateenies can perform in it before they leave."

"Count me in," said Emily. "I learned all about makeup this summer. I could be in charge of that. Oh, there's Mom, back from getting the mail. See ya."

Emily waved at her mother and ran toward the car.

"Emily looks different," said Noah, after she was gone. He looked down the driveway as the Dovers' car drove away. "She'd be cute in the circus."

Rats! thought Bailey.

12

Still No Captain

Sparrow stayed in her room all day with her door shut. Bailey wanted to go visit her, but Miss Bekka said it was better to wait. She said Sparrow needed alone time.

By late afternoon there were new worries. Captain Calliope had not returned. Mr. Will called the sheriff's department to find out if he had perhaps been in an accident. Miss Bekka called several stores in town to see if a man with big bushy sideburns had been there to buy supplies. No one remembered seeing anyone who fit that description.

"What will we do with the Goateenies, Dad?" asked Fred.

"They'll be fine. The captain left enough food to take care of them for several days. Go ahead and feed them supper. Maybe he'll be back in time for a late dinner," said Mr. Will. "He's new to the area and may be lost."

Supper. Bailey looked at her watch. Sugar would be fixing the evening meal, and she needed to get home to set the table. "C'mon, Goldie," said Bailey. "I'll be back tomorrow, everybody. Tell Sparrow hi."

"You bet," said Mr. Will.

Bailey grabbed Goldie's leash, and they walked to the familiar path in the woods that led to Sugar's house. Goldie sniffed the ground and trees, and perked her ears to listen to something Bailey couldn't hear. It was comforting to have Goldie walk with her. She hoped that soon she would be able to let Goldie off the leash when the hound could be trusted to stay by her side. That would require more training when Justin had time. He knew how to teach animals to behave and do tricks.

"I'm so glad you're my dog," Bailey said. She reached down and petted Goldie's head.

13

Home with Sugar

Bailey gave Sugar a big hug when she found her in the kitchen.

"We have lots to talk about tonight," said her grandmother.

"I guess," said Bailey. She looked through the mail pile to see if her mother had sent a new postcard. The only mail was Sugar's.

"Emily called again. She asked me to tell you that her slumber party is a week from Saturday. I told her I thought that would fine," said Sugar.

"I don't want to go," said Bailey.

"Oh?" said Sugar. "Any particular reason?"

"Just don't."

Sugar looked puzzled. "Well, Bailey, it's up to you. Just let her know." She opened the refrigerator. "It was too hot to use the stove today, so I made shrimp salad, and we can have ice cream and fresh peaches for dessert."

Bailey washed her hands and set the table.

"How's Sparrow?" asked Sugar.

"She wouldn't come out of her room," said Bailey. "I think she's worried that she might have to go away. Do you think that'll happen?"

"For our sake, I hope not, but the case-worker will be looking at what's best for Sparrow. We'll just have to see." Sugar placed her recipe book back on the shelf, then said, "You have time to check your e-mail before supper. You'll notice a bunch of papers on my desk next to the computer. I've been searching on the Internet for information about Captain Calliope. What I found is interesting. Bring the papers to the kitchen when you come."

"Okay," said Bailey. She opened the refrigerator to see the salad—one of her favorites. There was enough for two big helpings each.

"My search also led me to learn more about circus history. One bit of information always leads to new questions," Sugar said.

Bailey poured kibble in her pets' bowls and went into Sugar's office.

She glanced at the top piece of paper before she checked her e-mail. It was a long story about the captain. *I'll read it later,* she thought.

14

E-mail for Bailey

When Bailey logged on she found that she had three new e-mails. The first was from her mother.

From: Mollyf2@travl.net
To: "Bailey"<baileyfish@gmail.com>
Sent: 5:16 p.m.
Subject: school

Hi sweetheart: Sugar says middle school begins in three weeks. I bet you're excited. When I was a girl, they called it junior high, and it was only grades seven and eight. We thought we were so cool. I got to meet many new kids who had gone to different elementary schools. Sugar told me to be myself and always do the right thing. She's probably told you the same. I know you'll be fine.

Andrew was recently interviewed for a cable television network special. I'll let you know when it will be on--probably next spring. I was in the picture briefly, but it was all about him and the great research he's doing on insect specimens.

Absolutely amazing! We're going to celebrate at dinner tonight at our favorite little restaurant.

Girlfriend, I wish you were here to help me pick out a dress and brush my hair to get ready for my date. You always told me when my makeup was the right shade.

Miss you, but gotta run. Andrew will be here soon.

xxxooo Mom

Bailey covered her eyes. She remembered brushing her mother's thick, wavy dark hair that looked good no matter how she styled it. Sometimes Molly's lotions smelled like roses and other times like coconut. *I wish she didn't like Dr. Andrew Snorge-Swinson—Bug Man. I wish a crocodile would eat him in one big gulp,* Bailey thought. *Then Mom would finish her book about him and come home. Not in time for middle school, but maybe for Christmas and we'd be together again.*

Bailey opened the next e-mail in her inbox. It was from her half sister, Norma Jean, who lived with their dad in Guam.

From: pjfish2005@yermail.net>
To: "Bailey"<baileyfish@gmail.com>
Sent: 7:35 p.m.
Subject: Hi

What's been going on? I just sent you three pictures I drew after we went to the beach. The water was so clear I could see every shell and fish.

We started band practice yesterday. I get to be in upper grades marching band because they need more trumpets and I'm the best. I think we will march in the Thanksgiving parade at the base unless we move by then to the States. Write back and tell me what's happening.

Sisters Club Rocks

Norma Jean

Bailey smiled as she imagined Norma Jean marching down the street blowing her big trumpet. Her half sister was shorter than Bailey. With her creamy skin color and long shiny almost-black hair, Norma Jean looked more like her mother, Flora, than she did their father, Paul Fish.

When Bailey met Norma Jean and their father for the first time in the spring, she hadn't liked her half sister at all. But then they helped save the old house in the woods, before the Keswicks fixed it up and moved in. Norma Jean and their dad kept writing about coming back to the USA, but he hadn't gotten a new job yet. Meantime, there was so much to tell her about Captain Calliope and the Goateenies.

From: "Bailey"<baileyfish@gmail.com>
To: <pjfish2005@yermail.net>
Sent: 7:40 p.m.
Subject: Hi

There are new visitors at Keswick Inn. Captain Calliope, a circus guy, and his act came this week. The act is a goat named Gruff, a potbellied pig named Bunny, and a rooster named Caruso. The captain wants them to do tricks so he can go back to the show, but he has gone away and we don't know where he is. So we are taking care of the animals and training them. Sort of. They really don't want to do anything but eat.

Everybody is really worried because Sparrow might have to leave instead of being adopted by the Keswicks, like Noah and Fred.

Justin says hi. Is Guam hot now? Sugar's calling. Supper's ready. Bye.

Bailey quickly glanced at her best Florida friend's e-mail. Amber was planning a pizza party with their friend Ashley. Amber and Ashley both had birthdays on the same day.

Bailey decided to answer Amber later.

15

Early Circuses

"Captain Calliope's real name is Fred Harrison?" asked Bailey. She helped herself to a second portion of shrimp salad.

Sugar spread out papers she had printed out from Web sites. "Apparently so. Many performers go by special names—show names," said Sugar. "He probably took the name Captain Calliope because it had a circus sound. And apparently he is a distant relative of Frederick Harrison Bailey. That makes him a part of the famous Ringling Brothers and Barnum & Bailey Circus family."

"Wait. Wait!" exclaimed Bailey. "His family's name is really Bailey?"

Sugar smiled. "Seems so. It was a common circus name in the early years." She pushed her empty plate to the side and adjusted her glasses. She studied the papers. "What fascinates me is that Hachaliah Bailey, a distant cousin of Frederick, was also a circus man. He had a menagerie in Virginia, and he established Bailey's Crossroads, near Washington, D.C."

"Cool," said Bailey. "A menagerie? Is that like a circus?"

"Not really. A menagerie is more about animals being on exhibition—on display."

Sugar silently read on, then said, "About 200 years ago, Americans really liked looking at exhibits of strange animals, like camels, lions, and polar bears. In about 1808, Hachaliah displayed the second elephant to travel our country." Sugar turned the page.

"Here it says that the elephant was so popular that Hachaliah added tigers and other animals to his menagerie."

Bailey put the dishes in the sink. Her mind was dancing with questions.

"Did the menagerie animals do acts? What else does the article say?" Bailey tried to read over Sugar's shoulder, her chin touching her grandmother's soft, short, dyed-brown hair.

"No, back then most of the circuses and menageries were separate. Then, just before the Civil War, most had combined the animal and the people parts, such as acrobats, into a single show," said Sugar.

She adjusted her glasses again, read for a moment, then added, "What's more, many circuses today no longer have animals—just people doing incredible stunts. Some folks think that it's kinder to animals not to train them to perform."

"So what about Captain Calliope's family? What did they do?" asked Bailey

Sugar read on. "This article isn't very clear, but they had various connections to several large and small circuses. We'll do more research later." She handed Bailey the stack of papers. "Your friends might be interested."

Bailey nodded. She was thinking about Fred and Noah's plans for a backyard circus.

"I once heard a calliope on a merry-go-round," said Bailey. "It had gold pipes and sounded happy, but like it was out of breath. It was really neat."

"I have a CD of circus music. You're welcome to it," said Sugar.

"That would be fun to play when we do our show. If Captain Calliope comes back."

"What do you mean?" asked Sugar.

"He wasn't there when I left today," said Bailey.

"Hmm," said Sugar. "I hope nothing has happened to him."

"He seems really sad about something," said Bailey. "Maybe he misses the other Goateenies—the first ones. The ones that could perform the amazing tricks."

"You might be right," said her grandmother. "I guess we'll find out when he returns."

16

Upset

Bailey was late getting to Keswick Inn the next morning because Sugar needed help hanging sheets on the line to dry, and it was Bailey's day to vacuum upstairs. When she was finished, she put the stack of papers about the circus into an envelope to take to the boys.

Goldie was waiting for her by the back door. Bailey snapped the leash on the dog's collar and yelled, "Bye, Sugar."

"Have fun," called Sugar from the side yard where she was filling one of her many finch feeders.

As Bailey reached the Keswicks' yard, she saw Sparrow wheel her chair from the house down the ramp into the morning sunshine. The girl lifted one hand to wave, but didn't smile.

"Where're Noah and Fred?" Bailey asked.

Sparrow pointed to the barn. "Feeding Goateenies. They said I could help."

"That'd be fun," said Bailey, wishing Sparrow would look happier. "Which Goateenie do you like the best?"

"I like them all, but Gruff is my fave. His whiskers tickle," Sparrow said, but without her usual grin.

"Noah said we're going to start planning our circus today," said Bailey. "We're going to decide on the acts and who will do what for sure. Fred's going to make another list."

Sparrow didn't answer.

"Didn't you say you want to be the bareback rider?" Bailey asked.

"Yes, but I might be gone—" Sparrow stopped talking. She turned her face away.

"Don't be silly," said Bailey. "You'll be here."

"You don't know," said Sparrow. She turned and quickly rolled her chair toward the house.

"Wait, Sparrow. Wait for me!" called Bailey. Sparrow didn't wait. Bailey decided not to follow. It seemed as if the little girl wanted to be alone. Bailey knew exactly how that felt.

17

Caring for Goateenies

"Hey, anybody in here?" called Bailey. Her eyes hadn't yet adjusted to the dark barn. Golden ribbons of sunshine streamed through cracks between the barn boards, but they failed to light the large room with old stalls and pens. She heard Justin mumble, "Here, with Fern."

"I'm helping feed Bunny," Justin's little sister said.

"I'm here, too," said Fred. "Near Gruff's pen. Noah's taking corn to the rooster. Boy, can that guy crow! He woke me up this morning."

"I see you now," said Bailey. "I brought stuff about the circus. Sugar and I've been reading about it."

"So have we," said Noah. "It's our next homeschool project. The history of the circus." Noah started talking in his deep pretend-teacher voice. "Listen up, Miss Bailey Fish. Did you know that a small circus by the name of

Brown and Bailey took their tent to cities in Virginia in 1825–1826? Fredericksburg, Richmond, Lynchburg, Norfolk, Lawrenceville, the Shenandoah Valley, and eventually into Maryland and Pennsylvania? By the way, Bails, are you related to the circus Baileys?"

"I don't know," Bailey replied. "Mom never said."

"The tent shows went a lot of different places besides Virginia," continued Noah.

"Well, Sugar and I learned that Captain Calliope has circus and menagerie ancestors," Bailey said. "Hey, did he come back yet?"

"Nope. Not a word," said Noah. "I think Gruff misses him. He keeps climbing on the crates in his stall to look out the window."

"We also learned that the first menagerie included a mongoose, a monkey, and a tiger," said Noah.

"That's sort of like having a pig, a goat, and a rooster," said Bailey. She called to Gruff. He stared at her, but didn't get down off the crates.

"I wonder why Captain Calliope would leave the big circus for carnivals, fairs, and a little show. They mostly have rides and things like that—not acts," she continued.

"Don't know," said Noah. "Maybe he'll tell us when he returns. We'd better get to work cleaning up the pen before Dad gets back from town." He tossed an empty, dented bucket to Bailey.

"The hose is over there," Noah said.

Bailey filled the bucket only halfway to make it easier to carry and poured fresh water into Gruff and Bunny's drinking trough.

Noah and Fred were replacing the dirty straw on the floor with clean straw. They had little to say. Bailey knew they were worried about Sparrow. Everyone was.

"Sparrow's afraid she won't be here for our circus," Bailey said.

"I know," said Fred.

"I don't know how we can stop it," said Noah. "I just can't believe our sister might not be our sister." He kicked the empty bucket. Gruff jumped. "Sorry, goat dude," said Noah.

"I know! We could pretend she has the measles or something like that," said Fern very seriously. "I've got lipstick in my room. I'll go home and get it and we could make spots on her."

"But what happens when the 'measles' are over?" asked Noah.

"We could tell them Sparrow has a really bad cold," said Fern, "and has to stay in bed for a year."

"And after a year?" asked Noah. His face softened into a smile at Fern's earnest expression.

"Then we could hide Sparrow at my house," Fern said.

"There will be no hiding anybody, sweetheart," said Miss Bekka. Bailey and her friends turned in surprise. Nobody had heard the boys' mom come into the barn. "I know you all mean well, but we've got to hope that it will all work out for Sparrow, whatever is best for her. Understand?" Miss Bekka looked at each of them for a response.

Bailey nodded first.

Fred said, "But, Mom—"

"I know. I'm worried, too. But worry won't change anything right now, and we have things to do today at Keswick Inn besides caring for the Goateenies. Fern, maybe you'd like to help Sparrow and me paint the rocking chair Sugar picked up for us at a yard sale. Mr. Will needs Justin and the boys to work on fences. And Bailey, your grandmother called. She'd like you to hurry home for a little bit. Something has come up. She wants to talk with you."

Surprised, Bailey grabbed Goldie's leash and dashed for the door.

18

Not Happy News

Sugar was picking plump tomatoes when Bailey and Goldie ran into the yard.

"Are you okay?" Bailey asked as soon as she could catch her breath. Her freckles disappeared into her flushed face.

"I'm fine. Here help me with the basket. It's pretty full, and I don't want tomatoes to roll out," said Sugar.

Bailey dropped the leash so she could hold the basket with both arms. Goldie followed them to the house. "Good girl," Bailey said.

"What's up? Miss Bekka said you wanted me to come home."

"Come sit down and have lemonade," said Sugar. Bailey carefully placed the basket of fresh garden vegetables on the counter near the sink, then sat at the kitchen table. When Sugar had big news, she often took her time sharing it. Bailey figured the news must really be important or Sugar would have mentioned what it was right away.

Her grandmother poured pink lemonade with crushed mint leaves into two tall glasses, and pulled up a chair for herself.

"I had a call from your mom today," Sugar said. "Actually, she called to talk with both of us, but you were already gone."

"Mom? She called? Is she all right?" Bailey was afraid that something had happened to her mother. Maybe she was sick and needed them to come take care of her, or maybe she was leaving Costa Rica and coming home for good. Maybe she wanted Bailey to come for a visit. Bailey's mind raced. Her thoughts almost drowned out her grandmother's answer.

"Well, you know your mother. Molly's always full of surprises. I don't know how exactly to say this. She said the other night when she had a celebration dinner with Dr. Andrew Snorge-Swinson, he asked her to marry him."

Bailey's eyes opened wide. "Mom said no, didn't she?"

"Actually, she said yes," Sugar answered.

Bailey felt like she was spinning into a dark pit. She heard Sugar calling her name as she knocked over her chair, ran out of the kitchen, and up the stairs. She threw herself on her bed and buried her face in her red, white, and blue quilt. She felt Goldie's warm, wet tongue licking her hand. Then Sugar's arms sheltered her. "It's okay, Bailey. It's okay. We'll talk whenever you are ready."

Bailey rolled over, sat up, then buried her face in Sugar's denim shirt. Sugar rocked her back and forth, humming softly.

"Did she really say yes?" whispered Bailey.

"Apparently so. Molly sounds very happy," said Sugar, patting Bailey's hair.

"I hate Bug Man," Bailey finally said. "And he doesn't like me. And he doesn't like cats and dogs. He's allergic. I don't like him at all."

"I know you don't," said Sugar.

"But how can Mom like him? Can't she just write books and articles about him? She doesn't have to marry him." A sob caught in Bailey's chest.

"It's hard for kids to understand why their parents fall in love with people they might not like," said Sugar.

Bailey pulled back. "What else did she say?"

"Well, they're hoping you'll be the maid of honor."

"They're planning a wedding?" The words stung as she said them. "When?" It seemed like a bad dream.

"In about six months," said Sugar. "I told her I would tell you everything, and then you two can talk about it. We can call her later today," said Sugar.

"I don't want to talk to her," said Bailey, surprising herself. She closed her eyes.

When Bailey was a little girl, she dreamed of being a bridesmaid in her mother's wedding. Bailey imagined exactly what her new father would be like. He would be handsome, have a sense of humor, and would be delighted to have Bailey as his new daughter. He would even love Bailey's cat, Barker. The three of them would have lots of fun together. He would not be like Bug Man, with his ponytail, thick glasses, and allergies. Bug Man spent his life studying bugs, for heaven's sake.

"And, what about me?" Bailey asked. "What did she say would happen to me?"

Sugar sighed, gave Bailey another big hug and walked over to the dormer window.

"She hopes you'll want to live with them," said her grandmother. "But that's a later conversation. A lot can happen in six months or a year. Meanwhile, I want you to know I love you. I will always love you."

Bailey hugged Sugar, then put her arms around Goldie. "And I love you, too."

"I'll be downstairs if you want to call your mom," said Sugar.

"Not now," said Bailey. She wrapped herself in the quilt and closed her eyes. Goldie stretched out beside her.

19

More E-mail

Sugar was sitting by Bailey's bed when she woke up. "I fixed your favorite sandwich for lunch—peanut butter and raspberry jam. Hope you don't mind," said Sugar.

"Sounds good," said Bailey. "I didn't mean to sleep."

"Sometimes a nap is just what's needed," said Sugar. "I snooze once in a while myself."

Bailey sat up and ran her fingers through her mussy hair. "I guess I'm hungry," she said.

"Good," said her grandmother, "because I also made triple fudge cake—my grandmother's special recipe."

"You're the best," said Bailey. She knew Sugar was trying to cheer her up.

"I'll be in the kitchen," said Sugar. "It'll be a couple of minutes."

Bailey decided to check her e-mail. She hoped to hear from Amber about her birthday.

It was the first time Bailey had missed her friend's party since they had met when they were little.

There was no message from Amber, but there was one from her mother.

From: Mollyf2@travl.net
To: "Bailey"<baileyfish@gmail.com>
Sent: 1:05 p.m.
Subject: Need to talk

Dearest Bailey, I'm sorry that you weren't home when I called this morning to share my news. I had hoped that you would be happy for me, for us, and would have called so we could talk. But Sugar e-mailed that you are upset. I know your visit last spring with Andrew wasn't as good as I had hoped, but I think in time the two of you will get along fine. He felt just as uncomfortable meeting you as you did with him. I simply want all the people I love to love each other.

We have much to talk about. Please stop pouting and give me a call or at least e-mail me.

Love and kisses, Mom

Stop pouting? Bailey couldn't believe her mother had written that. She wasn't pouting. She was upset and not in any mood to discuss anything with her mom. Not yet.

Bailey wanted to tell Norma Jean and Amber. They might understand. But maybe they wouldn't. Norma Jean would be all excited about the wedding. Then she would tell their father, and he would want to find out what was going on. Bailey didn't want to talk with him about her mother's plans, either.

She decided to go back to Keswick Inn after lunch. Maybe at supper Sugar would say that Molly had called again and had decided that she wouldn't marry Bug Man after all because Bailey was more important to her than he was.

The peanut butter oozed between the slices of wheat bread as Bailey took a large bite. Sugar looked at her face and said, "Did you get an e-mail from Molly?"

Words were stuck with peanut butter in Bailey's mouth.

"You know, I think it's important to tell her how you feel—when you're ready, of course," said Sugar. "It's hard when you're a kid and the person you're talking to is an adult, but your mom needs to know how you feel."

Bailey didn't answer.

"If I can help, let me know," her grandmother said. "Everything's going to be fine."

Bailey took a big gulp of milk. *Why can't Mom be more like Sugar?* she wondered.

20

Grooming Gruff

"C'mon, Goldie," she said. Bailey decided to let the dog follow her without the leash. Goldie stayed by her side through the woods.

"You're such a good girl," said Bailey. "I know you care. Mom'll really like you when she sees you someday." Goldie's tail wagged into Bailey's knee.

Fred and Justin were fast-walking Bunny and Gruff in a large circle when Bailey returned. Bunny sat down and grunted. She wasn't pleased at the exercise even though she wanted the piece of carrot that Fred held out for her.

Gruff had also had enough. When he saw that Bunny had stopped walking, he tried to slip out of his collar. "No, you don't," said Justin. "It's okay." He scratched Gruff's chin.

"I don't think they want to be in the act," said Fred.

Justin said, "It takes patience to train an animal. Repetition and reward. Repetition and reward. You do the trick over and over, and the animal learns. On TV I've seen pigs play ball and dogs ride on skateboards."

"Yeah, but these dudes aren't doing much, even with rewards," said Fred. "When he gets back, maybe we should tell Captain Calliope that he needs different Goateenies."

Justin shrugged.

"If the captain shows up," said Bailey.

"Where've you been?" asked Fred. "I thought you were coming right back to help."

"I wasn't gone that long," said Bailey.

Noah came out of the barn with a soft grooming brush. "Hey, Bailey, what's up? What'd Sugar want?"

Bailey didn't answer. She pretended to be adjusting Goldie's collar.

Noah handed the brush to her. "You can groom Gruff while we work on enlarging the Goateenies' pen."

Bailey said, "Okay." She wondered if she should say anything about her mother's awful plans. Fred and Noah were her best friends, but she wasn't sure what to tell them. Instead, she looked at the brush. "What do I do with this?"

"Hang on to Gruff's collar, then brush him gently," said Noah. "That's what Captain Calliope told me to do."

"Will Gruff bite?" asked Bailey.

"Nah, hasn't yet, but sometimes you've got to watch his head," said Justin. "He might butt a little."

Gruff studied her and wiggled while Bailey held his collar tightly. She was glad to have something to do.

Fred tied Bunny's long rope to a tree. "Keep an eye on her," Fred told Bailey. "Dad said that we should make their barn stall open out into the yard so they can go outside when they want to. So we've got to make an outside fence. C'mon, bro," he said to Noah.

"The Goateenies will like that," Bailey said.

21

A Talk

Bailey crouched down and stroked Gruff's soft hair. The little goat nudged her cheek. Bailey put her arms around Gruff's neck and smiled.

"I'm glad to see you smiling," said Miss Bekka. "I saw your sad face when you came back from lunch with your grandmother. Is everything all right?"

Bailey hadn't heard the boys' mother walk over to the apple tree. She was so startled that she lost her balance and plopped down.

Bleh. Gruff trotted away as far as his rope would allow and nibbled on tender grass.

"You surprised me," said Bailey. Her face turned as pink as Goldie's tongue.

Miss Bekka sat down on the lawn next to her. She leaned back against the tree. "Would you like to talk? I'm a good listener," she said.

Bailey pulled her knees up under her chin. She really wanted to tell someone about her mother and Bug Man, but was afraid of what she might say and how it would come out. It was all so confusing.

Miss Bekka pushed loose strands of her long, dark blond hair behind her ears, then stroked Goldie, who was lying by Bailey's side.

"I guess so," Bailey finally said.

Miss Bekka waited.

"My mom's going to marry Bug Man," Bailey blurted out.

"How does that make you feel?" asked Miss Bekka softly.

"Really mad," said Bailey. "I hate him."

"Oh," said Miss Bekka. "Any particular reason?"

"Lots of reasons," said Bailey. "He's weird. He doesn't like my animals or me."

"And he's taking your mom away from you?" Miss Bekka asked quietly.

Bailey couldn't control the hot tears. She quickly wiped her eyes and buried her face between her knees.

Miss Bekka put her hand on Bailey's shoulder.

"I don't want to be in the wedding. I want Mom to give back the ring," Bailey whispered.

"Are you worried about what might happen to you?" asked Miss Bekka.

Bailey nodded.

"May I hug you?" asked Miss Bekka.

Bailey nodded again. Miss Bekka's hug was soft as a baby blanket.

"You know, Bailey dear," Miss Bekka said, "when I was a little girl, my parents were divorced, and my mother met a man and married him a few years later. It was quite an adjustment for all of us. At first I liked him and then I didn't and later I did."

"Yeah, but he isn't Bug Man," said Bailey. "I don't like him. You don't know him."

"That's right. I haven't met Andrew—Bug Man," said Miss Bekka. "You know, that is a great nickname for a man who studies bugs." She laughed. "Bug Man," she repeated, and laughed again.

Bailey smiled and said, "I guess it does sound funny."

Miss Bekka looked at her watch. "Oh, it's time to put the bread in the oven, and I have to help Will fix a fan—I'm the chief electrician in the family."

"Really? Sugar's our electrician," said Bailey. "She's teaching me all kinds of things."

Miss Bekka stood up and held out her hand to Bailey. "Have you talked with your mom?"

"No."

"I think it would be a good idea to tell her exactly how you feel," said Miss Bekka.

"That's what Sugar said, too."

"Think about it," said Miss Bekka.

Bailey looked away, past the fruit trees, where the field ended and the woods began.

She nodded.

22

More Planning

"Step right up! Circus planning time," shouted Fred, in his best ringmaster voice. He was waving his yellow pad. "C'mon to the chicken coop," Fred called again.

Bailey wiped the corners of her eyes and stood up, brushing grass off her shorts.

"Coming," she called back.

"Now," said Fred, when everyone arrived, "it's time to do some serious planning if we're going to have the circus before your school starts. Noah and I are always in homeschool, but the rest of you gotta get on those yellow buses in a couple of weeks."

"Okay," said Noah. "Will we have a tent?"

"That would be kinda hard to make, a big one, I mean," said Bailey.

"We could use sheets," suggested Sparrow.

"We'd need a lot of sheets," said Fred, chewing on his pencil.

"Miss Bekka has tons of them in the linen closet," said Sparrow. "All different colors."

"We can ask her," said Noah, "but we could have the circus under the apple trees."

"That would be easier," said Fred. But after he looked at Sparrow's face, he added, "Maybe a tent might work and we could use the clotheslines. The acts could be under the tent and the people could sit under the trees."

Sparrow smiled.

"Next," said Fred, "admission. What should we charge?"

"Fifty cents," said Fern.

"A dollar," said Noah.

"That's a lot," said Bailey.

"I'm thinking half will go for buying our chickens, and the rest for the town food bank," he said. "And we'll share our brown eggs."

"Fine with me," said Bailey. She brushed an ant off her ankle.

"Mom'll like the eggs," said Justin. "But what about the animal acts? The Goateenies aren't ready, and they don't like learning tricks."

"We've got a lot of work to do with them," said Fred, "but we can plan our other acts, like the acrobats. That's what I want to write down now. All the things we're going to do."

"And what we're going to sell. Sugar and I could make popcorn," said Bailey.

"See if you can get Goldie and Clover to act like lions," said Fred.

Goldie rolled on her back. She didn't look very fierce. *Oh well,* thought Bailey. *People will just have to imagine that she is the queen of the pride.*

"You know, dudes," said Noah, "we don't have to have the circus before public school starts. We could have it on a Saturday anytime, whenever we're ready."

"No!" said Sparrow loudly. "It's got to be soon, because I want to be in it! You can't have the circus without me." She pounded her fist on the arm of her chair.

"We won't have the circus without you," said Fred.

"You're going to be the star," said Bailey, trying to sound like she meant it, but the sudden silence showed that everyone was concerned about what might happen to Sparrow after her aunt's visit in two days.

23

Sparrow's Aunt

"I'm really scared," said Sparrow. "I don't want to meet her." Sparrow's long, dark-blond hair hid her face.

"Everything'll be fine," said Bailey, even though she wasn't sure.

"Do I look okay?" Sparrow's voice seemed too small for her body. "I hope she doesn't like me. I hope she goes away."

"Miss Bekka says she's probably very nice," said Bailey.

"Stay with me."

"Sugar says I have to wait outside while you meet her. Goldie and I'll be by the big apple tree."

Sparrow brushed back her hair and nodded.

Bailey looked at her watch. It was 1:55. She heard Miss Bekka calling Sparrow to come to the porch. Sparrow stuck out her chin and slowly rolled the wheelchair through the door of her room. Bailey followed, then went down the steps and walked to the apple tree where Goldie was tied. She threw her arms around her dog. "Don't let them take Sparrow, please," she whispered into Goldie's neck. The dog tensed as a van came up the driveway and parked near the house. Goldie growled a quiet warning.

Bailey turned to watch. The passenger's door opened. Josie Parker, Sparrow's caseworker, got out with a large canvas briefcase. She took off her sunglasses and tossed them inside the van. The side door slid open, and a woman in a wheelchair was lowered to the ground on what looked like a little elevator. Bailey couldn't have been more surprised. Sparrow's aunt was also in a wheelchair? Bailey wondered what Sparrow would think.

The woman released the chair's brakes and started its electric motor. She followed Mrs. Parker up Sparrow's wooden ramp to the porch where the Keswicks and Sparrow were waiting.

Bailey could not hear what anyone was saying. She saw Miss Bekka motion to everyone to sit down. She saw Fred go into the house and return with a tray of brownies.

Bailey looked at her watch. Sugar had said she would come over after she had received a call from Miss Bekka that the visit had ended. That could be a while.

She heard a *bleh*. Gruff wanted company. Bailey said, "C'mon, Goldie, let's go see Gruff and Bunny."

As her eyes adjusted to the dark inside the barn, she saw Justin. "I didn't know you were here," Bailey said. "I thought you were baby-sitting your sisters today."

Justin rubbed Bunny's leathery ears. "Sparrow," he said. He sounded worried.

Bailey nodded.

"Want to help me work on the tricks?" Justin asked.

"Sure," said Bailey. She was glad to have something to do to forget about the terrible visit that was going on.

"Watch this," Justin said. He squeaked the rubber duck. Bunny quivered with excitement and looked at him. "Sit, Bunny," Justin said. Bunny sat down.

"Wow!" said Bailey. "How did you get her to do that?"

Justin actually smiled. "Patience and practice. Repetition and reward. I've been spending time with them every day. Now watch this."

He untied the rope that held the gate closed on Gruff's pen and led the goat into Bunny's nearby enclosure.

"Pyramid," Justin said quietly.

Bunny dropped her short legs so she was flat to the ground. Justin put a blanket on her back and repeated the command. Little Gruff carefully stepped on Bunny's back. He bent his left front leg and put his head down.

"It looks like he's bowing," said Bailey.

"You got it," said Justin. He smiled again and gave each animal a piece of carrot.

"What about Caruso? Did you put him on top yet?" she asked.

"Not yet. I want them to get used to each other first."

"Captain Calliope will be so amazed," said Bailey.

"If he comes back," said Justin.

"He wouldn't abandon the Goateenies," said Bailey.

"People do."

"But the Goateenies are famous," she said.

"Not these Goateenies. They're new. They're not the famous ones," Justin said. "And they only do the pyramid when they feel like it. You're lucky you saw it."

"Cool," said Bailey.

"I'm going to teach Gruff to count to ten," said Justin. "Lots of animals do that in shows."

Bailey sat on a bale of straw and watched Justin turn a bucket upside down. He petted Gruff for a long time, then said, "Now you're going to count. He picked up Gruff's front leg and tapped it on the bucket. "One," Justin said.

Bailey's mind wasn't on the training. She wondered what was happening on the porch. Was everyone crying? Was Sparrow packing? Would she be allowed to say good-bye to her friends? Would they ever see her again?

Just as her worries bubbled like a pot of boiling water, Bailey heard Sugar calling her name. "Bailey, where are you? You can come here now."

"In here, Sugar," called Bailey. Justin quickly closed Gruff's pen and hurried toward the barn door with Bailey.

Sugar was on the screen porch steps. The van with the wheelchair lift was still parked next to the ramp.

"Come inside, you two," said Sugar when she saw Justin was with Bailey. "The Keswicks want us to meet Sparrow's aunt."

24

Aunt Coco

The first thing that Bailey noticed was that everyone was smiling. What was going on? Wouldn't somebody be unhappy?

Aunt Coco and Sparrow's wheelchairs were parked side by side.

"This is Aunt Coco," said Sparrow. "She's really nice, like they said."

Bailey was afraid. Did that mean that Sparrow would be leaving with her?

Bailey looked around at everyone. She had never seen such big smiles on Fred and Noah's faces. Mr. Will looked as if he had won the lottery, and Miss Bekka was beaming.

"Okay," said Sugar. "Don't keep us in suspense."

Aunt Coco said, "I'm sorry to have caused such concern. I hadn't seen Sparrow since she was a teeny baby and went into foster care. I always wanted to care for Sparrow, but my own health has been a problem. When I heard she was about to be adopted, I wondered if I could manage raising her. I had no idea what the adoptive family was like, so I wanted to see for myself." She looked at Sparrow and put her big hand over Sparrow's small one. Sparrow squeezed it.

Aunt Coco continued. "I now know this is the best possible home for my niece. I can see that the Keswicks are wonderful people. And, what makes them even more special is that they have assured me that Sparrow and I may visit each other whenever we want." Sparrow grinned at her aunt.

"You can't have enough good people in a family," said Mr. Will.

"Look what Aunt Coco gave me," said Sparrow. She held out a fleece lap blanket. "She says it will keep my legs warm in the winter. She has one just like it."

Bailey felt Sugar's arms surround her with a huge grandmother hug.

"So now I will have a forever family and an aunt," said Sparrow. "Right, Miss Bekka?"

"You betcha," said Miss Bekka. "When can we expect a court date?"

"These things take time, Bekka," said Mrs. Parker, "but I'll start the paperwork when I get back to the office. Are you ready to go now, Coco?"

"I guess so," Aunt Coco said reluctantly.

"Come back," said Sparrow.

"I will, little one," said Aunt Coco. She leaned across the wheelchair arms and kissed Sparrow's forehead.

"And you can come to our circus," said Sparrow.

"I'd love to," said Aunt Coco. "I'm very good at cheering, and I know the story of the elephant ballet."

"An elephant ballet? What's that?" Sparrow asked.

Aunt Coco looked at her watch and Mrs. Parker.

"Go ahead. I have a few calls to make," said the caseworker. "If you'll excuse me." Mrs. Parker walked outside to the yard.

"Now close your eyes, everyone, and imagine this scene," said Sparrow's aunt.

25

Modoc and Zorina

"It's a true story—about the elephants," Aunt Coco began. "My very own mother was at the Ringling Brothers Circus in Madison Square Garden in 1942."

"Really?" asked Bailey.

"Yes. Now, I want you to keep your eyes closed and imagine this. Fifty elephants wearing pink tutus enter the arena.

"With them are fifty beautiful ballerinas, also dressed in pink. Can you see it? They perform to music by a very famous composer named Stravinsky. A very famous choreographer—that's someone who creates the dances—worked with him. His name was Balanchine."

Aunt Coco paused. "Sparrow, you're peeking. You're supposed to be imagining."

"I am imagining," said Sparrow. She scrunched her eyes closed again.

"Mother told me that a ballerina named Zorina rode on the trunk of Modoc, a young elephant. Modoc was the biggest elephant in the show. The music was grand. There was a special polka. You can open your eyes now."

"That must have been wonderful," said Bailey.

"Oh, yes," said Aunt Coco. "My mother loved to tell the story, and she made a scrapbook about it. She said there were more than 400 performances."

"I know! We could have an elephant ballet in our circus," said Sparrow.

"We don't have any elephants, little sister dude," said Noah.

"What about the Goateenies?" asked Bailey.

"Bunny and Gruff, and especially Caruso, wouldn't wear tutus," said Noah.

"I mean, *we* could pretend to be the elephants and the ballerinas," said Sparrow. "Close your eyes and imagine it." She grinned.

"I'll be one," volunteered Miss Bekka.

"We all will," said Sugar. "And I'll get the pink net fabric when I go to town."

"Forget it. Not me," said Justin. He crossed his arms and leaned back against the wall.

"Ha," said Sparrow. "I think you would be cute in a tutu." Justin shook his head no, but he was smiling at Sparrow.

Mrs. Parker poked her head in the door. "Ready?"

"So soon? I guess," said Aunt Coco.

"Please come anytime," said Miss Bekka.

"Only if I can be in the elephant ballet, too," said Aunt Coco. "I can do some pretty fancy moves in this chair." She spun it around.

"Cool," said Sparrow.

26

Another E-mail

"That was a wonderful surprise, wasn't it," said Sugar, when they arrived home. "We've a lot to be thankful for."

"I really like her aunt. I hope she comes back for the ballet," said Bailey.

"I think she will. I'm going to run into town for groceries and the mail. Want to come?"

"Sure," said Bailey.

"Give me a minute. I need to make a list," said Sugar. "By the way, Mrs. Dover called this morning to say she hoped you'd change your mind about the sleepover. She said Emily'll be disappointed if you don't show up. You're one of her best friends."

Bailey still didn't want to go, but she finally said, "I guess I will." She couldn't come up with a good reason to stay home.

While her grandmother made her grocery list, Bailey wandered into Sugar's office to check e-mail. The only one was from her mother. Bailey wasn't sure she was ready to read it.

From: Mollyf2@travl.net
To: "Bailey"<baileyfish@gmail.com>
Sent: 1:45 p.m.
Subject: sorry

Bailey, I wish you would talk with me. I apologize for using the word "pout." I know you don't like that word, and it wasn't fair of me. Andrew and I do care about how you feel, but unless we talk, how can we tell you that? Please let me know when you'll be home and ready for a phone call. I'm also going to talk with Sugar about getting Webcams for each of us. That would be fun. I love you, sweetheart.

xxxooo Mom

Bailey hesitated. She was about to ignore the message, but she remembered what Sugar and Miss Bekka had said about talking it out.

Bailey clicked REPLY.

Hi, Mom.

Her fingers stopped typing. She stared at the screen.

We're going to have a circus. Remember when you rode the elephant and Amber and I were there?

Her fingers stopped typing again.

I miss you.

She erased that.

When are you coming home for good? Love, Bailey.

She added:

Your daughter.

She hit SEND.

27

Slumber Party

"I'm glad you changed your mind." Emily threw her arms around Bailey. "Hey, everybody, Bailey's here!"

Emily pulled Bailey's green knapsack out of her hands and led the way to the living room. She put it on top of all the bags and sacks that the other girls had brought. Bailey knew most of the guests, but they were the "popular kids," the group that Emily wanted to hang out with.

Emily's little brother, Howie, popped up from behind the couch and waved at Bailey.

"Hey, Howie," Bailey said.

He quickly put his finger to his mouth to shush her, but Emily spotted him. "Howie Dover! Out of here or I'm telling Mom."

"Okay. Okay," he said. He yanked Emily's hair and hopped on one foot out of the room.

"Brothers," Emily mumbled. "I've got to help Mom." She went to the kitchen.

Bailey stood awkwardly by herself in the doorway between the dining room and the living room. After the girls had initially said hi, they turned back into their circle. Bailey listened while they chatted about what they had done that summer and what they were getting for school. They had traveled to places she had never heard about, and were buying jeans and tops with unfamiliar brand names.

Bailey had outgrown her clothes with designer labels that she wore in Florida. Her mother liked to shop at the mall and buy the latest fashions for both of them. Sugar was much thriftier and bought Bailey's new clothes at discount stores or on sale at outlets. Emily's friends probably knew the difference just by looking at hers. Bailey wished she had worn her best shorts to the party instead of her old white ones.

Although all the girls were talking at the same time, Sierra's voice was the loudest and soon had everyone's attention. Bailey couldn't understand why anyone liked her and listened to her. Sierra was stuck up and mean. Here she was, the loudest and the leader.

Every once in a while, one of the girls would look at Bailey, but no one invited her to join them. Bailey's feet felt glued to the doorway. She could hear Emily and her mother in the kitchen. Should she go help them, or should she try to join the party? She remembered what Sugar had told her. Sometimes you have to face your fears and try to fit in. Your impressions of people may be wrong.

Bailey forced her feet to walk toward the circle. Sugar was right. The girls made room for her between Tammi and Hannah. Sierra stopped talking and sized up Bailey. Then the tall girl said, "So, what did you do that was cool this summer?" Her voice had a mocking tone, like she would pounce on whatever Bailey said and play with it like a cat with a toy.

"My friends and I, well, we had a play. My cousin came to visit, and we're planning a circus."

Bailey was immediately sorry that she had said anything. It was all so much fun with Noah and Fred and Sparrow, but she could tell from Sierra's hard look that she thought it was stupid. Bailey's cheeks were as red as spaghetti sauce.

"A circus?" said Sierra slowly, as if she were imagining Bailey as a gawky clown. Sierra raised her eyebrows. "How juvenile."

The other girls laughed. "I suppose you'll be in one of the acts, Bailey. We'd love to come," said Sierra. She looked around at the giggling girls.

"When will you have the circus?" Sierra persisted.

Bailey didn't answer.

"We have to train the Goateenies first," said Emily. She was carrying a tray piled high with hot dogs in buns. There were enough for two for each person. She placed them on the dining room table.

"Goateenies. Now that's *really* funny," said Sierra with a snarling laugh. The other girls laughed again.

Bailey waited for Emily to tell her friends that she wanted to be in the circus, too, but Emily was suddenly silent. She gave Bailey a look that said, *Don't you dare talk about it now.*

28

Mess

"Come and eat. Supper's on the table," announced Emily. "Mom said you can eat anywhere you want, but try not to spill."

Bailey waited until the other girls were helping themselves before she went to the end of the line. Emily's little sister, Nannie, refilled the bowl of pickle chips and gave Bailey a big smile on her way to the kitchen.

At least someone likes me, thought Bailey. She carried her cup of soda and paper plate with a hot dog and chips back to the living room. All the seats were taken, so Bailey sat on the floor near the dining room doorway. Before Bailey could take a bite, Sierra jumped up and said, "I'm getting more chips." She brushed past Bailey, stepping on Bailey's hot dog. Soda spilled all over the plate and floor.

"Oh, sooo sorry, circus girl," said Sierra, as the others laughed. "You could feed this mess to the Goaties, or whatever you call them." She smirked as she left the room.

Bailey's shorts were splattered with catsup. She picked the pieces of smushed hot dog off the rug and looked around for help. She felt as small as the pickle chip on her mashed plate.

Nannie had seen what happened. She hurried to the kitchen to find her mother.

"It was just an accident," said Sierra sweetly when Mrs. Dover came in with towels and a bucket of soapy water. Mrs. Dover bent down to wipe up the mess.

Nannie said, "You did it on purpose."

"Enough of that, Nannie," said Mrs. Dover. "Sierra is our guest."

Nannie put her hands on her hips and stared at her mother's back.

Bailey stood up.

"If you'd like me to wash your shorts, dear," said Mrs. Dover, "just change into your jammies now. And there are plenty more hot dogs."

Bailey hesitated. She wasn't hungry anymore, and she didn't want to be the only kid wearing pajamas at supper.

She decided to try to wash out the catsup spots in the bathroom.

"Thanks, I'll be okay," Bailey said.

"I'll help you," said Nannie.

Emily was nowhere to be seen.

~ ~ ~

The splatter marks didn't rub out of her white shorts very well. They were now surrounded by gray blotches of water.

"I look really stupid," said Bailey.

Nannie asked, "Do you want me to get you some of Emily's shorts?"

"No. I'm all right. Thanks, Nannie."

"Sierra is really mean. She's mean to Emily, too, but Emily is afraid of her and won't say anything. She thinks Sierra will be her friend."

Bailey hadn't thought about that. She had just figured that she was the only one that Sierra picked on. She didn't know what to do. Sugar would say, "Be brave. Be a Wild Woman." Her mother would say, "Don't let people bully you. Don't follow the crowd just to be popular." Bailey didn't feel very brave.

Bailey hugged Nannie. "I'm ready. Let's go." She opened the bathroom door.

Sierra was watching for her. The tall girl stared hard at Bailey's shorts, then sneered.

"Hey, look. You could be a leopard in the circus, with all those spots."

Be brave. Bailey took a deep breath and said, "I'm the great catsup leopard of Lake

Anna. Very rare." Bailey saw Sierra look at her in surprise. Bailey felt bolder. "Rare and fierce," Bailey added. Nannie giggled.

Sierra didn't smile. She turned back to her friends. For a moment, Bailey thought the nastiness was over, but she heard Sierra say, "Guess what? Bailey is already in her circus outfit." And she heard someone say, "I guess she's the clown?" and the laughing burned her ears.

"Time for makeup," called Emily. "I set things up in the family room. Follow me."

"Do we do each other or ourselves?" Monika asked when the other girls rushed after Emily.

"Each other," said Sierra. "I want to do Bailey. You don't mind, do you, catsup leopard princess?"

Bailey shrank under the older girl's gaze. They were the only ones left in the hall.

"I don't like makeup," said Bailey, taking a step back.

"You'll like mine." Sierra pulled a tube of bright red lipstick from her pocket, popped off the cap and before Bailey could get away, smeared it all over her face.

Bailey jerked back against the wall. Sierra wasn't done. She made red dots on Bailey's light blue shirt.

Just then Nannie appeared. She took one look at Bailey and ran for her mother.

Mrs. Dover said, "Oh, my, what happened? Nannie, go get your sister."

Sierra said, "Just a little accident. Bailey isn't used to makeup, and I was trying to help her. Sorry." She gave Bailey a warning look and went into the family room.

Mrs. Dover said, "I had trouble learning to use makeup, too, when I was your age. Emily, bring my cold cream and a towel."

Bailey said, "I'd like to use your phone, please."

"Sure, hon, as soon as we wipe you up," said Mrs. Dover.

Emily returned with the makeup remover and the towel. Her eyes showed worry. "You're not calling Sugar, are you?" she asked.

Bailey nodded yes. "I'm going home."

"You can't leave. Sierra will make fun of you all night."

"I don't care."

"You won't say anything, will you?" asked Emily.

Bailey didn't answer. She dialed Sugar's number.

"I'll be right there," said her grandmother without asking any questions.

29

Comfort

Sugar didn't ask questions on the drive home either. She had brought Goldie with her, and Bailey buried her face in the dog's soft neck.

The phone was ringing when they reached Sugar's front door.

"I'll get it," said her grandmother.

Bailey went into the bathroom to see if all the lipstick was gone from around her eyes. The faint red circles made her eyes look as angry as she felt. She scrubbed her face until it was pink and shiny, then turned her T-shirt inside out, trying to hide the worst spots until she could change.

"That was Emily's mother," said Sugar when Bailey came out of the bathroom. "She figured out what happened and is dreadfully sorry. Sierra has been sent home. Mrs. Dover would like you to come back for the rest of the party."

Bailey shook her head no.

"That's what I told her. I said you were brave to put up with the bullying as long as you had, and that I was proud that you called me."

"I was only a little brave," said Bailey. "I stood up to her, but then she made fun of me again."

"Well, it's not good for Sierra to get away with these things. Mrs. Dover and I are going to have a visit with her parents."

"No!" said Bailey, with alarm.

"It won't be just the two of us. We're going to talk with the parents of the other girls, too. I think they've all had problems with her."

Bailey was quiet. She wondered what would happen when school started. Sierra would be there, mean as ever. She'd be out to get Bailey for sure. Maybe Sugar would let her stay home and go to homeschool with the Keswicks. Suddenly, she realized that Sugar was talking to her.

"I haven't had supper yet, and there's plenty for the two of us."

Bailey's stomach told her that it would welcome food. "Sure, after I change," she said.

"Let's both wear jammies," said Sugar.

"Deal," said Bailey.

30

Porch Talk

After supper, Sugar said, "Let's sit on the porch a while. The crickets are singing tonight."

Shadow and Sallie were curled up on the smooth wooden steps. Goldie lay down near Bailey's purple rocker, careful to keep her paws from being rocked on.

Bailey leaned back in her chair and put her feet on the wooden railing, just like her grandmother was doing.

"Hear the owl?" asked Sugar.

Bailey nodded. "The owl reminds me of Florida. There was a nest near where we stayed at the Sanibel beach," she said.

She grew quiet, remembering how one night she and her mother listened to the owl from their balcony, then Molly said, "Girlfriend, look how bright the moon is. Let's walk on the beach."

Bailey said, "I'll be ready in a minute."

"No, we're going in our nightgowns," said Molly, tossing back her thick dark hair. "We'll run until we're out of breath, then we'll make a big sand castle, then we'll have cookies and milk and go to bed. Race you."

Molly always had such fun, crazy ideas. Why did she go away? Didn't she remember running on the beach as they stepped on ouchie shells and sloshed through the waves? Didn't she remember when they saw a giant sea turtle digging in the sand to lay her eggs in the moonlight? Didn't she remember the next morning when they saw the nest had been roped off by the turtle patrol? Molly told her how lucky it was to see the turtle. Didn't Mom remember anything?

"Bailey, you seem a million miles away."

"Sorry," said Bailey.

"I took a big step this afternoon," said Sugar.

Bailey stopped rocking.

"We're getting satellite Internet, which is expensive, but it means we can have a Webcam."

"A Webcam?" asked Bailey.

"It's a little camera that hooks into the computer. When two people far away have them, they can see each other when they talk." Sugar paused and looked at Bailey. "Now we'll be able to visit with your mother in person."

Bailey was quiet. Then she thought, *Maybe if Mom sees me, she'll want to come home, and it'll be just the two of us again.*

"Good," said Bailey.

"I'm glad you think so," said Sugar. "Now, I'll have to figure out what to wear during our first video chat—certainly not my jammies."

31

Good Friend's Offer

Sparrow stuck a carrot through the boards of the new outdoor pen. Gruff trotted over and grabbed it before Bunny could get there.

"Here's another one for you," Sparrow said, and dropped it through the fence right by Bunny's front feet.

Bailey heard her say, "I wish you were my Goateenies. I hope Captain Calliope never comes back."

"I wish they could stay, too," said Bailey. "We all like them."

Sparrow brushed her bangs out of her eyes and held out a piece of apple to Gruff. "I like him a lot. I like him better than the rooster. He might peck me."

"Caruso doesn't peck hard," said Bailey. "Where're Noah and Fred?"

"They're helping get guest room number six ready for people"

"What people?" asked Bailey. Room six had never been used for guests, just for storage. She knew the other guest rooms were "occupied," even if the people who rented them were away, like Captain Calliope.

"Nobody right now, but Miss Bekka wants to get it ready in case more guests come. She says we're getting really popular."

"Maybe we should help," said Bailey.

"You can. I'm going to visit with Bunny," said Sparrow.

When Bailey reached the back porch, she could hear Miss Bekka say, "Now that the boxes are in the attic, we need to set up the twin beds and make sure the dresser drawers are wiped out and everything is spotless."

"I'll help," Bailey said, stepping inside.

"Thanks. You could cut zinnias for the hall table. Fresh flowers look so nice."

Bailey knew where Miss Bekka kept the garden scissors. She took them to the flower bed and made sure she had left long stems on each of the colorful flowers. She arranged them in the tall pottery vase that Miss Bekka had set out near the sink.

Mr. Will called to Noah, "Okay, just one more set of springs and a mattress. Bailey, if you're done, you can help Fred."

"Sure," she said.

Fred was struggling with a bedspread, trying to make all the sides the same length. Bailey tucked it in under the pillow and smoothed the top.

"Thanks," said Fred. "Hey, I heard that Emily's friends were pretty mean to you."

Bailey's face grew hot. "How'd you hear that?"

"Justin, I think. He knows a lot of stuff."

Bailey wasn't sure what to say. She didn't want Fred and Noah to think she'd been a baby at the party.

Fred wiped a smudge off the mirror over the dresser. "You're our friend. We'll defend you, if you need us," he said, pretending to box.

"Just call on the Super Keswick Twins. Pow! Pow!"

Bailey grinned. "You're the best," she said.

How could I ever have thought they would like Emily more than me just because she looks cute with makeup? she wondered.

Sparrow returned from the barn. "We've just got to work on the circus," Sparrow said. "And we haven't done the Goateenies today. You know, train them."

"Okay," said Fred. "Let's go *do* them." He grinned at Sparrow.

Bailey quickly followed. Fred hooked Bunny's leash to her collar and led her into the yard. He had her rubber duck in his pocket.

Fred said, "Sit, Bunny." The pig sat, although it was hard to tell that her back end was down because she was so short.

"Duck, Bunny," he said, while Bailey and Sparrow watched. He placed the rubber duck on her large snout. Bunny snorted and the duck fell off.

"I'm beginning to think this is hopeless," said Noah. He had brought Gruff out of the barn. "No wonder Captain Calliope abandoned them. They aren't interested in doing tricks except sometimes for Justin. But they don't do them all the time."

"How will we have a circus, then?" asked Sparrow, about to cry.

"We can always do something else," said Bailey.

"No! Aunt Coco said she'd be in the circus. We've got to have a circus," said Sparrow. "You promised."

Bailey looked at Noah and Fred.

"We'll think of something," said Noah.

"We can still do the elephant ballet," said Sparrow. "And Goldie will be the lion, and you can be a clown."

Noah rolled his eyes.

"Sugar said she was going to buy pink netting for the costumes," said Bailey. "We could at least have the elephant ballet and the other acts, like juggling."

"Nobody here juggles," said Noah. "We'll think of something else."

32

Webcam

"The circus is Saturday, but we don't know what we're going to have besides the elephant ballet," Bailey told Justin. He had come over to help Mr. Will build an outside pen at the chicken coop. The rooster would then be able to go in and out of the chicken house and find bugs and worms in the enclosed grassy area.

"Figures," said Justin. He didn't seem surprised, but he looked disappointed. "It takes time to train animals. They're just starting."

"Maybe you can lead them in the parade," Bailey said.

"Nuh-huh," said Justin. "Not me." He wandered toward the chicken coop where Mr. Will was unrolling the wire.

Bailey looked at the piece of paper Fred had written out for her. Her instructions were to make sure Sugar had the material for the costumes. She and Sugar were supposed to make fliers to put up around town to let people know about the circus. It seemed like a lot to do in just a few days. *Without a real show, what's the point of the fliers?* Bailey wondered.

Miss Bekka said she would contact Aunt Coco to see if she could come early to practice the ballet.

With everyone busy at Keswick Inn, Bailey decided to go home with Goldie. When she reached the backyard, she saw that a satellite dish had been installed. The metal dish was tipped up to face the southwest sky.

Her grandmother was at the kitchen table looking at a small black object with a cord.

"It's our Web camera," Sugar said, when Bailey gave her a hug. "I'm trying to figure out how to hook it up." She handed Bailey the directions.

Bailey read through the booklet, then said, "I'm not sure, but it looks like this cord hooks in the back of the computer, but we also have to install the right program with a CD. See?" Bailey handed the directions back to Sugar.

"Hmm. Between us, I think we can figure this out. Let's try."

A few minutes later Bailey and Sugar could see their faces in a little box on the monitor. It was like looking in a computer mirror.

"Now," said Sugar, "we need to come up with a special screen name to use when we're online, and we need to find out your mother's screen name."

While Bailey watched over Sugar's shoulder, her grandmother typed a note to Molly using Bailey's e-mail address.

From:"Bailey"baileyfish@gmail.com>
To: Mollyf2@travl.net
Sent: 4:15
Subject: Chat

Hi Molly: Bailey and I are inviting you to a video chat. Let us know your screen name, and when we might get together tomorrow. We're done with the computer for today.

Love, Sugar and Bailey.

Sugar hit SEND.

"Now, let me show you the tutus I've made," Sugar said.

33

Surprise Storm

Bailey could hear Sugar's clock bonging six times. Or was it five bongs and . . . a clap of thunder? She sat up quickly in her bed. Lightning crackled across the sky, and there was another boom. It sounded close, as if the lightning had aimed directly at a tree in Sugar's yard. She looked around for Goldie. All she saw was a long tail with a white tip sticking out from under the bed.

"Don't worry, Goldie girl. I know the booms are scary, but don't be afraid," said Bailey. However, her heart was pounding from the surprise early morning storm. Rain slapped her dormer window. The hall light, that Bailey liked to leave on at night, flickered and went out. Bailey's room was dark.

"What a storm," said Sugar, coming into Bailey's room with a flashlight. "I knocked on your door to see if you were awake, but I don't think you heard me over all that racket." She closed the dormer window and wiped up the rain on the windowsill with a towel.

Bailey was really glad to see her. Another giant clap of thunder sent Shadow and Sallie into Bailey's closet.

"Glad I made my coffee before this wildness came over the mountains. I don't think the weather forecasters were expecting this," said Sugar.

Bailey slipped a robe over her pajamas.

"It seems colder, too," said Bailey.

"That happens when the fronts come through. Look, it's hailing."

White icy pellets hit the window so hard that Bailey worried that they would break the glass.

"Hope the hail doesn't ruin the tomatoes," said Sugar. "Let's go down and see what we can scrounge up for an early breakfast."

"C'mon, Goldie," Bailey called gently. Goldie thumped her tail, and wiggled backwards until she was out from under the bed. Bailey had no luck coaxing the cats out of the closet. All she could see were shiny eyes at the very back behind her winter boots.

"I think the whole neighborhood is without power. The phones are out. I tried calling Miss

Bekka on her cell phone, but just got her voicemail," said Sugar.

Bailey stepped out on the back porch when the rain seemed to let up. The sky was still darker in the west, and the sunrise was stalled in the east. Then the wind and rain started up again, but they were not as fierce as during the first part of the storm.

Sugar's cell phone rang. "Oh, that explains it," her grandmother said. "No, we're fine."

Sugar snapped the phone closed. "Will said a huge tree fell across the road and took down the power lines. He called the electric company, but it may take time to clear the road and restore power."

She studied her cell phone. "Unfortunately, I didn't put it on the charger last night. Not much battery left."

Another boom that echoed across the lake convinced Bailey that there was no point in walking to the Keswicks until the storm had passed. She poured kibble into Goldie's bowl. Her dog was usually right at her side when she was fixing breakfast for her pets, but not right now. Goldie whimpered and huddled in the broom closet.

"You're such a scaredy cat, I mean, scaredy dog," she said to the trembling hound.

"I hope your mom won't try to reach us this morning to video chat, because we can't use the computer for a while," said Sugar.

"And without power, we can't do the laundry, or use the vacuum, or make toast," said Bailey with a grin.

"We can't run the water, either, because the well pump needs electricity to operate. But we can read," said her grandmother. "I found several books about the circus that you might find interesting."

"Sure," said Bailey, even though she really wanted to find out what was going on at Keswick Inn.

Goldie followed her to Sugar's library and sat on Bailey's feet, like a big furry slipper. The dog put her head in Bailey's lap and whimpered. The wind grew more furious. Sugar looked out the window. "Goodness, the leaves are twisting like dancers!" she exclaimed.

Bailey pushed Goldie aside and joined her grandmother. The rain was so heavy that Sugar and Bailey couldn't see the bird feeders hanging on a tree limb near the back porch.

"Wow! This is like the storms in Florida," said Bailey. She jumped closer to Sugar at the next flash. There was an immediate *boom*, then a huge cracking *thud*, then a terrible *thump*.

"Uh-oh," said Sugar. "I think something hit the house. We'd better have a look."

Bailey shivered. She and Goldie followed Sugar from room to room, searching for the source of the crashing noise.

"Oh, no!" gasped Bailey when they reached the upstairs hallway. A tree limb had fallen across her dormer. Rain was pouring into her room and dripping from the leaves that dangled through the crack in the dormer roof.

"I don't think it's safe to go near the dormer," said Sugar, holding Bailey back. "We'll move everything we can easily reach into the hallway."

Sugar pulled the quilt off Bailey's bed, and Bailey filled her arms with books that had been on a shelf near the doorway and pushed them into the hall. She couldn't see *Charlotte's Web* beneath the wet leaves in her dormer. The broken branch had covered her chair and table with an unwelcome green blanket. Bailey could hear the tulip poplar tree creaking above her; its branches were scraping the shingles, like a rusty hinge. She was afraid that more limbs might fall on the house.

"I think we've got what we can safely reach. Let's go back downstairs until after the storm," said Sugar. Her short hair and face were wet with droplets of rain. Bailey's robe was damp. She wished she had snatched clothes out of her drawer to change into. *I guess I'll take some dirty ones out of the laundry basket to wear today,* she thought.

Then she remembered Sallie and Shadow. "My cats! They're in the closet. We've got to get them!"

Before Sugar could say anything, Bailey rushed back in her room to her closet. The tree limb groaned again, and the hole in the dormer roof creaked larger.

"Be careful," Sugar said. "I'm behind you."

Bailey crawled on the damp closet floor. "Shadow? Sallie? Where are you?" Bailey pushed her shoes and boots out of her way. "Don't hide. Come out," she cried.

"Do you see them? We need to get out of here," said Sugar.

Bailey shoved aside a heavy box of sweaters near the winter boots. Behind it were two sets of eyes.

"They're here," Bailey said. She grabbed Shadow and handed him to Sugar. Then she picked up Sallie, who struggled to get away and hide again. "We're going downstairs. Now!"

As soon as they were out of her room, Bailey shut the door so the cats couldn't run back in.

124

Rain continued to pound on the windows and there seemed to be no end to the thunder and lightning.

"Darn," said Sugar, looking at her cell phone. "The battery is really low. I hope I can get through to the Keswicks." She dialed their number, but the phone peeped and went dead.

"What are we going to do?" asked Bailey in a small voice. She was trying not to think about her smashed-up room.

"As soon as the storm is over, we'll go to Keswicks and get help. I know you're worried, but everything will be okay. Rooms can be fixed, sometimes better than new."

Bailey's eyes filled. "Not everything. I had a box with all my mother's postcards in the dormer. I bet they're ruined. And pictures. And your special book, *Charlotte's Web*. I'm sorry. I promised to take care of it."

Sugar gave her a big hug. "The most important thing is that we're all safe."

"I know," said Bailey, shivering.

34

Neighbors to the Rescue

Noah and Fred were raking up the leaves and branches that had fallen during the storm when Bailey and Sugar arrived. Mr. Will hurried over to greet them.

"Pretty wild," said Noah. "Clover was so scared she hid behind the couch and whimpered. We couldn't reach her."

"Our power's still out," said Fred. "Good thing we have lots of candles and lanterns."

"I have a tree in my dormer," Bailey told them.

"Really?" said Fred. "Need help raking your room?"

Bailey grinned. "It's a bigger mess than your yard."

"We're okay at my house," said Justin, "but the road is completely closed by that big tree."

"Then we'll have to walk through the woods to cover your roof," Mr. Will, told Sugar.

He went into the barn and came out with a large piece of blue plastic. "You boys carry this tarp, and I'll get other supplies after I check on the animals to make sure they're safe." He disappeared into the barn, then quickly returned.

"All is well with the Goateenies," said the boys' father. He handed a box of tools to Noah and a small chain saw to Justin. "Let's go."

Bailey and Sugar followed the work procession through the woods. The brush along the path was still dripping. The little creek had overflowed its banks. Everyone had to wade through it.

"Wow!" said Fred, when he saw the large tree branch on top of Bailey's dormer roof. "Look at that!"

Mr. Will studied the tree and said, "We'll get Sugar's ladder and cut off the branch as much as possible. I think the tree itself can be saved. It's just leaning a bit. Then, after I have a chance to look at the damage, we'll cover the hole with the tarp."

Bailey watched from a safe distance. Thunder still rumbled in the north, but the storm seemed to have gone by, except for passing showers. As sections of the branch were cut off and crashed to the ground, she could see more and more of her dormer. The window glass was broken. The red café curtains with white stars that Sugar let her pick out at a store were torn and hanging like a flag on part of the branch.

"We'll get new ones," said Sugar. "The mall store might still have these in stock. Everything will be fine. You'll see."

It didn't take long for Mr. Will and Justin to board up the window and cover the damaged roof with a piece of blue tarp to keep out rain and wildlife. Fred and Noah carried away the pieces of branches.

"We should be able to replace the window and do the repairs after I have a chance to go to town for the right supplies," Mr. Will said. "It won't be difficult."

"I'd like to see my room," said Bailey, "if that's okay."

"I don't see why not," he said. "Sugar and I'll come with you."

"I want to see, too," said Fred.

"We're all going up," said Noah.

The room looked worse than Bailey had expected, but also better. Wind had blown papers everywhere. The branch had put a gash in the cushion of her reading chair and knocked her books and postcards to the wet dormer floor, where Mr. Will warned her not to walk just yet. Bailey worried that *Charlotte's Web* and her box of special postcards had been ruined. She couldn't see them.

"You're right, this is a mess," said Fred, while they examined the dormer from inside.

The pictures of her Florida cat, Barker, and her mom had fallen off her dresser, and the glass in her mom's picture frame had cracked.

"We'll replace that," Sugar said, giving her a hug. "Not to worry."

With the cracks in the glass, Bailey couldn't tell if her mother was smiling or if she had a faraway look, as if she wanted to leave on an adventure. It was getting harder to remember her mom before she left. Bailey carefully placed the photographs back on her dresser.

The family Wild Women.

She was surprised and happy that the pictures of the family's adventurous and brave

Wild Women were still hanging and undamaged. Their expressions seemed to tell Bailey to be strong and unafraid. She smiled back at them.

"You can sleep in the guest room tonight," said Sugar.

"Okay," said Bailey. She glanced at the Wild Women one more time before closing her bedroom door.

35

Goateenie News

The Keswicks invited Sugar and Bailey to eat at their house—with everything cooked on the grill. The electricity came back on after supper was served.

Suddenly the refrigerator hummed again, lights popped on in the kitchen and hallway, and a radio blared down the hall in one of the rooms.

"What a relief," said Miss Bekka. "I was afraid the food in the freezer might spoil if we didn't have power soon." She passed the bowl of potato salad to Bailey.

"So, are the Goateenies learning their tricks?" Sugar asked.

"Not too well," said Fred. "I don't think they'll ever be an act. I mean, I can't see them ever working together."

"Captain Calliope believes in them, and so do I," said Sparrow, passing the catsup.

Fred gave her a long look and said, "But he abandoned them."

"Did not!" said Sparrow, glaring.

"What do you call going off and leaving them then?" asked Noah.

"He's just busy somewhere. I know he'll come back," Sparrow insisted.

"We'll see," said Sugar. "I hope so."

"Coco said she'd be here about eleven," said Miss Bekka.

"She wants to be in the ballet, even if we don't have a circus this time," said Sparrow. "I'm going outside."

Just as she reached the door, the phone rang. "I'll get it," she said. She lifted the receiver to her ear. "It's for you, Mr. Will. I think it's Captain Calliope." Sparrow smirked at Noah.

Mr. Will took the cordless phone into the living room. Everyone grew silent around the kitchen table, except for Goldie who was thumping her leg while she scratched her neck.

Fred sneezed. "Shhh," said Noah, even though no one could hear their dad's conversation.

In a few moments, Mr. Will returned to the kitchen. "Sparrow was correct. That was Captain Calliope."

"What did he say, Dad?" asked Noah.

"Well, he'll be back on Saturday."

"Did he say where he's been?" asked Miss Bekka.

Mr. Will shook his head. "No, just apologized for worrying us and said he's on his way. I didn't get the feeling that he's planning on staying, though. He wants to know what he owes us."

Sparrow's face flushed with worry. "He's not going to take the Goateenies away. Not before the circus." She wheeled her chair toward the door.

"They belong to him, little one," said Mr. Will kindly.

Sparrow slammed the door behind her.

"Time for us to head out, too," said Sugar.

Bailey, Sugar, and Goldie walked home through the woods. Bailey carried a box flashlight to beam the way. The rain had called mosquitos to come out, and the woods were thick with them. Bailey and her grandmother swatted their arms and legs, trying to brush away the biting insects.

"We should have sprayed ourselves with insect repellent," said Sugar. "By the way, I had a message on my cell phone from Mrs. Dover. She was wondering how we came through the storm. She also said that Emily is extremely sorry about what happened to you at the sleepover, but she doesn't know how to make up with you."

Bailey slapped a mosquito that landed on her arm. "Got it," she said.

"Any thoughts?" asked Sugar. She missed a mosquito that landed on her nose.

"About what?" asked Bailey.

"About making peace with Emily."

"I don't know," said Bailey. She thought for a few minutes. "I mean, I'm not saying I'll never be friends again, but I can't really trust her. She does some mean stuff, or lets it happen." Bailey hopped as she reached down to slap a whining insect that had landed on her knee.

"I don't blame you for feeling hurt and betrayed," said Sugar.

Bailey thought about some of the fun times they had had. Maybe Emily hadn't planned for Bailey to be picked on.

"Maybe," said Bailey. "Sometime." She scratched an itchy spot on her arm.

"I'll tell her mother you're thinking about it, if that's okay," said Sugar. "Look, there's the porch light. Let's run for it. Go!"

Bailey and Goldie raced to keep up.

36

Video Chat

The answering machine was blinking when they got inside. Bailey hit the message button. The voice was a bit crackly, but there was no mistaking it: her mom.

"Bailey, Sugar, I've been so worried. At first I couldn't get through at all, and now that your phone seems to be working, nobody's home. Is everything okay? I'm ready to do the Webcam. How about tonight at eight your time?"

Sugar looked at the battery-operated kitchen clock. "Eight Eastern Standard is seven Central time in Costa Rica, and it's almost eight now. Goodness, we've never tried the camera program. What do you think, Wild Woman?" She looked at Bailey, who was still staring at the answering machine as if she expected her mother to pop out of it.

"I guess," said Bailey, shrugging. Her heart was pounding. She wanted to see her mother, but she wasn't ready. It had been so many months since Molly had stopped by for dinner with Bug Man in early spring.

"I'll go turn on the computer," said her grandmother.

Bailey filled the water bowls for her pets and looked at the bathroom mirror. She didn't have time to change into nice clothes or fix her hair. Her hairbrush and good clothes were buried somewhere in the mess of the room. *What will Mom think? She always looks so perfect.* Bailey's heart pounded harder.

"I hear a funny noise—like someone is trying to reach us," called Sugar. "I need help to figure this out."

Bailey splashed water on her face and quickly dried it. She patted water on a strand of hair that was sticking out.

By the time she reached Sugar's office, she could see her grandmother's face in a small box on the screen. Then all of a sudden a bigger box appeared. In it was her mother's face. It wasn't as clear as a television picture, but Bailey could still see her mom and her beautiful dark wavy hair falling on her shoulders.

"Sugar? I can see you. Wow! This really works!" said Molly. "Can you see me?"

"Indeedy," said Sugar. "You look terrific!"

"Where's Bailey?" asked Molly. "I don't see her."

Sugar moved her chair sideways. "She's coming in the door now." Sugar motioned to Bailey to pull up another chair and to sit in front of the camera.

"This is what I've been wanting," said Molly, "to see my baby girl. It's almost as good as seeing you in person. How ya doing, girlfriend?"

Bailey had to smile. Her mother looked so excited and happy. "I'm fine. Guess what? We had a bad storm and a tree hit my dormer," she blurted.

"You're okay, aren't you?" asked Molly. She peered into the camera, perhaps trying to see if Bailey was hurt. "Your hair looks different. Does it need cutting?"

"I'm fine, and my room's going to be fixed soon. Mom, do you want to meet Goldie?" Bailey reached for her dog and lifted her front legs up so that Goldie was in view of the camera. "Here she is." Bailey gave Goldie a kiss on the gold spot on her neck.

Instead of looking at Goldie, Molly turned and motioned to someone out of view. Bailey let Goldie slide back down to the floor.

"Andrew's here. He wants to say hi," said Molly.

"Bug Man," Bailey whispered under her breath. Dr. Andrew Snorge-Swinson, with his ponytail, wire-rim glasses, and pale blue eyes, bobbed into view.

"Hello again, Sugar and Bailey," he said cheerfully.

Bailey gave a small wave and Sugar said, "Good to see you, Andrew."

He smiled and looked around. "I've got to go. A little more work to do before we have dinner with friends. I know you girls have a lot to talk about."

Bailey could see his hand rest on her mother's shoulder. *How dare he? The creep.*

Her mother smiled as Bug Man disappeared. "He's so wonderful," she said.

"Oh, I want to show you my ring." She moved her hand directly in front of the camera. The ring was a white blur.

"Very nice," said Sugar. "The diamond looks quite large."

"It was his mother's," said Molly. "A real keepsake. Very special." She moved her hand back to the keyboard and twisted the ring.

I hope the diamond falls out and gets eaten by an iguana, thought Bailey, even though she knew it wasn't nice.

"So, don't you want to know about our wedding plans?" asked Molly. Whenever she moved, her face looked as if it were made of hundreds of little boxes, as if she were part of a video game.

"Mom, would you like to see Shadow and Sallie? They've gotten really big since you were here," said Bailey.

"You should see the three-toed sloth that hangs upside down from a tree branch outside the porch. There's so much wonderful wildlife here," said Molly. "What were you saying?"

"Nothing," said Bailey. She could hear a doorbell ring in the background.

"Oh, dear, those are our friends. They're early," said Molly, looking at her watch. "Been great talking with both of you. We'll chat again soon."

"Bye," said Sugar.

"Bye, Mom," Bailey said softly. The screen was already dark. Her mother was gone.

37

Wishes

Bailey decided to sleep in the guest room where her half sister, Norma Jean, had stayed in the early spring when she visited from Guam. Bailey's own room was still too much of a wreck, and she was too tired to straighten it up. She stretched out on the small bed. Goldie curled up with her head on Bailey's shoulder.

"You're so pretty," said Bailey. "Such a good girl. I'll never leave you. Never." Her mom could have that rotten Bug Man. Then she'd be sorry when she realized what he was really like and how much she missed her only child, Bailey. And she'd get on the Webcam and tell Bailey that she was coming home without him. The wedding would be off. She would put that ring on one of the sloth's three toes and toss her wedding dress into the Pacific Ocean.

Bug Man would be shocked and horrified, especially when he saw the sloth creeping off into the rain forest with the keepsake diamond glittering through the trees. He would try to talk Molly into staying, but she would say, "I've been terribly wrong. I must return to Bailey and Sugar. And that's that!"

Bug Man would offer to give up all his insects, but Molly's bag would be packed, and one of their friends would be waiting to take her to the airport.

Bailey sighed. As much as she wished her mother would come home to her, Bailey realized more than ever that her mom was happy in Costa Rica, engaged to Bug Man.

Bailey wished she had turned on the ceiling fan before she went to bed. The air was still and hot, and Goldie's breath was warm. She wished she were in her own bed, where cool night air came through the screen in the dormer window and the pictures of the Wild Women kept watch over her. But now the window was all boarded up, and her special possessions were a soggy mess.

At least I have Goldie, Sugar, and my cats, thought Bailey. She wrapped her arms around the dog and listened to an owl as she closed her eyes.

38

Apology

"Where's Sparrow?" Bailey asked Fred when she arrived at Keswick Inn the next morning.

"She's worried that the Goateenies are going away, so she's trying to teach Gruff and Bunny tricks for our circus. But I don't think we're going to have the circus now." He wiped his glasses on his yellow T-shirt.

"Why not?" asked Bailey. She followed Fred into the barn.

"Dad and Justin have loaded up the pickup with supplies to fix your room. Noah is supposed to help Mom clean the inn today, and I've got barn duty."

"But can't we practice later?" asked Bailey.

"Later is too late," said Fred. He picked up a shovel. "You can help me, though."

"Sure," said Bailey grabbing a broom.

They found Sparrow in the pen that housed Gruff. "Look, he's giving me kisses when I tell him to," she said. "Watch this. Kiss me, Gruff," she ordered.

The goat leaned close to her and put his mouth on her cheek.

"How did you get him to do that?" asked Bailey in amazement.

"Peanut butter," said Sparrow. "I put a teeny blob on my face, and he wants it. Neat, huh?"

Gruff leaned in again. "Wait," Sparrow said, "I haven't put more peanut butter on my face. You have to wait until I tell you to kiss me."

Bleh. Gruff backed away, then he trotted over to the stack of wooden crates Mr. Will had placed in a corner for him to climb on.

"Justin can get Bunny to sit when he tells her to," said Sparrow. "Maybe the Goateenies don't do the tricks that Captain Calliope wants, but they do tricks for us."

Fred finished shoveling out the dirty straw from the pen, and Bailey tossed fresh bedding on the floor. The dusty chaff made her sneeze. She flicked little pieces of straw from her arms and sneezed again.

"Next, the pig," said Fred. He was covered with pieces of straw.

"You look like the scarecrow in Oz," said Bailey.

Fred brushed straw off his hat. Bunny squealed loudly from the next stall. "We're coming," said Fred. He handed a small container of food to Sparrow. She placed it on her lap so she could use both hands to wheel her chair to Bunny's pen.

Bunny's fat snout pressed against the opening. Her leathery ears flicked. Sparrow lifted the board that kept the gate to the pen closed. She rolled in so she could place the food in Bunny's dish. The pig grunted happily. Fred cleaned Bunny's stall, and Bailey tossed fresh bedding on the floorboards.

Sparrow opened the spigot and let the water spill into Bunny's dented bucket. "If we don't have the circus, then Aunt Coco might not come back soon," said Sparrow. "She promised."

"I'm sure she'll visit anyway," said Bailey. "Sugar has made the costumes for the elephant ballet. We'll at least do that part of the show." She picked up another armload of straw.

"Maybe," said Fred. He and Sparrow were finished with their chores and leaving the barn.

"Did I hear my name?" It was Sugar.

What's up? Sugar doesn't usually come in the barn, Bailey thought.

"Hi, Emily," said Sparrow. "Where've you been?"

Emily? Bailey froze. *What's she doing here?* She turned and saw Emily walking a few steps behind Sugar.

"Someone wants to talk with you for a minute, Bailey," said her grandmother.

Bailey was too surprised to say anything. She put her hands on her hips.

"Mom brought me to your house, but you weren't home," said Emily. Her long dark curls were pulled back with a hair band, and her eyes looked worried.

"I'll leave you two alone for a few minutes," said Sugar, "while I go see Miss Bekka."

"I'm sorry, Bailey," Emily said. She looked as if she were afraid Bailey might yell at her. "I didn't stop them when they were mean."

Bailey didn't like surprises like this. Straw spilled out of her arms.

"If you don't want to be friends anymore, well, okay," said Emily. "But I'm not going to hang out with Sierra or any of the mean kids."

Emily sounded scared and sad.

"And I'm sorry about your room. I heard about the tree hitting it. If you need help—"

Bailey wanted to tell Emily how much she hated her party, but Emily already knew.

"Maybe you'd like to be in the circus, if we have it." Words slipped out of Bailey's mouth before she could stop them.

"Great! I can do makeup. Oops, sorry, no makeup," Emily looked worried again.

"It's okay to have makeup in the circus. It's going to be on Saturday," said Bailey. She grabbed a broom and swept up the spilled straw. Emily bent down and picked up loose pieces and put them on the pile in the corner near Gruff and Bunny.

"Oh, wait. I can't come. We're going to be out of town on Saturday," said Emily.

"Well, thanks about my room," said Bailey. "We need to get more curtains—at the mall."

She smiled a little smile to let Emily know she was trying to be friends again, too.

A car horn honked.

"That's Mom. See ya," said Emily.

"Bye," said Bailey, but Emily was already out the door.

39

More Imagining

At lunch time, Bailey wanted to return home to see how things were going with the roof. Sugar said they should both stay out of the way until the main outside repairs were done.

"Besides, I have tutus for everyone in the truck, and I thought we'd see how they look," said her grandmother.

"For everyone?" asked Bailey.

"You'll see," said Sugar. "There must be some surprises. Now help me with the boxes."

Bailey carried the smaller one and Sugar a large one. "Let's take them to the barn," said her grandmother, "near the circus props. Now see if you can round up your friends."

Fred was in the kitchen making his special brownies with Sparrow, while Noah was vacuuming the hallway. Bailey tapped him on the shoulder. "When you're done," she yelled over the noise, "c'mon outside."

"Five minutes," Noah signaled, holding up his hand.

Soon her friends were done with their chores and arrived at the barn.

"Okay," said Sugar. "Tutus for everyone."

"Not me," said Fred. "If we have the circus, I'm the ringmaster, remember?"

"I'll do it," said Noah. He took one out of the box marked LARGE. "Hey, this is huge," he said, holding it up.

"It's not for you," said Sugar. "That one's for Bunny, and there's one in there for me. Look at the name tags."

"Here are ones for Sparrow, and Gruff, even Clover and Goldie," said Bailey. "I guess we're all elephants or ballerinas."

"What about Aunt Coco?" asked Sparrow.

"A special one for her," said Sugar. "Now, according to the picture I have of the Ballet of the Elephants, Modoc went first. Who wants to be Modoc?"

"I do," said Sparrow. "No, wait. I want to be the ballerina with Modoc."

"I'll be Modoc," said Noah. "This is too simple. So, we line up and parade around? Then what? This isn't going to be much of a show. In fact, I don't think we should invite anyone. We'd have to give their money back."

"Listen to this," said Sugar. She pushed a button on her boom box. "It's the 'Polka for a Young Circus Elephant' that was written for the original act. It's not very long, about four minutes, but that should give us plenty of time to be silly." The music started.

"Now, everyone close your eyes, listen, and like Aunt Coco said, use your imagination," said Sugar. "What do you see?"

The music made Bailey imagine huge, gray elephants trying to dance lightly with their heavy feet. She heard them trumpet to each other while the circus band played the modern-sounding dance music. The elephants were twirling and lifting graceful ballerinas with shimmering pink dresses high in the air. All too soon, the polka was over. Bailey wanted to hear it again.

"Then what?" repeated Noah. "What will we do after the ballet thing? The Goateenies haven't learned much, and we've been too busy to work on anything else. We might as well give it up."

Fred nodded. "Agreed."

"But Gruff kisses me when I tell him to," said Sparrow.

"And I saw Bunny sit down when Justin to her to," added Bailey. "And I saw Gruff stand on Bunny's back for at least ten seconds. It was almost a pyramid."

Noah rolled his eyes. "Big deal," he muttered. "It's time to call it quits, dudes."

Miss Bekka put on her tutu. "I think this is charming. Sparrow is right. We need to have the ballet. Aunt Coco will definitely be here, and we don't want to disappoint her. Now, back to work everyone. The brownies must be done by now, and the porches need sweeping."

"Oops," said Fred, "I forgot the brownies. I hope they didn't burn."

He ran for the kitchen.

40

Like New

By late afternoon, Mr. Will and Justin returned from Sugar's house.

"We're finished," said the boys' father. "Looks pretty good—at least from the outside."

Bailey gave Mr. Will a hug and thanked Justin. "You're the best," she said to them. She looked at Sugar.

"Sure, we can go back now," said her grandmother.

Bailey and Goldie were in the truck before Sugar could say, "Ready?"

When they turned up Sugar's driveway, Bailey peered out the window to see her dormer. The blue tarp was gone. Boards no longer covered the window. It looked as if nothing had happened, except for the old tree. It was now missing a huge branch. The branch had been cut into firewood and neatly stacked near Sugar's woodpile.

"Wow!" said Bailey. "It really looks good."

She hopped out of the truck, and Goldie scrambled to keep up as Bailey ran for the front door. Goldie brushed past her on the stairway and beat Bailey to the room.

Bailey opened the door and turned on the light. Mr. Will and Justin had even straightened up some of the mess. They had stretched out beach towels on the floor near the dormer window and spread out the damp postcards and books, including *Charlotte's Web* and her writer's notebook, on them to dry. "They should be okay," Mr. Will had told her.

The window was missing its curtains, and the dormer walls needed repainting, but her room didn't look too bad.

I can sleep in here tonight, Bailey thought. Goldie had already curled up in the middle of the bed. Bailey sat down next to her and rubbed her ears. *It's good to be home.*

Bailey heard Sugar call her from downstairs. "I just got an e-mail from your mother. She'd like to do a video chat in a few minutes."

Bailey went to the mirror and brushed her hair.

41

Another Video Chat

"Go ahead and visit with her while I fix supper," said Sugar. "Just hit that VIDEO button when you're ready." She patted Bailey on the shoulder and went into the kitchen.

Bailey watched the large black box on the screen change into her mother's face.

"Hi, Mom," she said. She tried to see what her mother was wearing. She didn't recognize the green sleeveless blouse or the silvery necklace.

"Oh, Bailey dear, this is so much fun to be able to see you. I don't feel quite so far away," said Molly. "Sugar e-mailed that the room is fixed up like new."

Bailey nodded. She saw that Shadow had followed her into Sugar's office, so she picked him up and put him on the computer table.

"Remember Shadow?" she said. The cat walked in front of the screen.

"I do, but now I can't see you. He's blocking the view." Bailey smiled and tried to make Shadow lie down, but he wouldn't stay. She finally had to put him on the floor.

"That's better," said her mother. "Did you brush your hair today? It looks kinda mussy. Remember I used to have to get after you before you went to school?" Molly laughed. "And you never wanted to get out of bed, either, especially in the summer, pumpkin. Are you still a sleepyhead?"

"I get up pretty early," said Bailey. "There's fun stuff to do here."

"Speaking of things to do," said her mom, "I'm going to talk to someone soon about my wedding dress. Andrew and I haven't set a date yet, but my friend Sylvia knows someone who can make whatever dress you want from just looking at a picture. I wanted to get your opinion. Which do you like the best?"

Bailey swiveled around in her chair so her back was to the camera. She gripped the arms of the chair, then rolled out of view.

"Bailey, where'd you go? Do you like this one with the sleeves, or this one with the flowered lace? Bailey?"

Bailey thought about what Sugar and Miss Bekka said about telling her mom how she felt.

There would never be a good time to do it. Goldie padded into the room and thudded down next to the door. Bailey could hear Sugar chopping vegetables in the kitchen.

She swung her chair around and wheeled it back to the computer. Her mother was waiting for her with pictures of wedding dresses.

"Which do you like?" Molly repeated. "I want you to be involved."

"Mom," said Bailey, taking a deep breath. "I don't want you to get married to Bug Man."

"What did you say?" Molly asked, putting the papers down. "I couldn't hear you."

"I liked it just the way we were, just the two of us," Bailey continued. She felt a little braver with each word. "Remember?"

Her mother was silent. They looked at each other without saying a word.

Finally, her mother said, "Bailey, I do love you. More than you could ever know. But I also love Andrew, and he's very good for me. We're very happy. In time, when the two of you get to know each other—"

Bailey sunk in her chair. "I don't like him. Can't it just be you and me again? I'll take care of you."

"What did you say? I think we've got a bad connection." The screen went blank.

Mom doesn't care, but at least I told her, Bailey thought, slumping in the chair.

"Supper's ready," called her grandmother.

Bailey turned off the computer. "Coming," she answered.

42

Captain Calliope Returns

Rats! It's Saturday. I overslept, thought Bailey. She looked at her clock. *I'll be late.* She slipped into her denim shorts and a light blue T-shirt with a picture of a yellow cat's face on the front and a brown dog on the back.

The air was cooler this morning. Bailey went to her dormer window for a quick look before grabbing her sandals. Sugar was pulling the newspaper out of the tube. She started up the driveway but turned back. Bailey saw Captain Calliope's truck slow down to a stop. Sugar walked over to talk with him.

"C'mon, Goldie, we've got to get to Keswick Inn before the Goateenies leave," Bailey said.

Bailey rushed downstairs and sat on a stool to fasten her sandals. She saw that Sugar had fixed a plate of toast for the two of them. She took a piece and folded it in half so she could eat it faster.

"Whoa, slow down, girl," said Sugar, coming in the door. "What's the hurry?"

Bailey shook her head. Her mouth was too full to talk.

"Well, Captain Calliope is back," said Sugar. "He stopped to say hello."

Bailey nodded and chewed harder, then gulped orange juice to wash it down.

"I know," she finally said. "I want to go say good-bye to the Goateenies."

Sugar said, "I understand. I'll be along. Coco is due there before noon."

Bailey hooked Goldie's leash on her collar, and they ran across the backyard to the path leading through Contrary Woods. The temperature was so much cooler that Bailey had a few goose bumps on her arms.

When they reached Keswick Inn, Bailey saw Captain Calliope talking to Mr. Will and the boys.

"I'm sorry I had you worried," said the captain. "Thanks for taking care of all of them."

"The kids did a great job," said Mr. Will. "You're welcome to come back anytime."

"That's what I wanted to talk with you about," said Captain Calliope. "You see—"

Suddenly there was a loud thumping from within the truck. He thumped back on the door.

"You see," the captain continued, "I was able to locate the original Goateenies. Ruben, Bella, Finch, and the lovely Zola Mira. We've worked out our problems. We're an act again. The real Great Goateenies. You should see their tricks!"

Captain Calliope beamed, causing his bushy squirrel-tail sideburns to wiggle. He opened the back of his truck. Three large goats with long horns peered out of their traveling pens. One was black with a white spot on its nose, another was gray, and the third, brown.

"Meet Ruben, Bella, and Finch," said Captain Calliope.

"Where's Zola Mira?" asked Mr. Will.

"She'll be along soon. She stopped for gas. All is forgiven. We're friends again."

"But what will happen to the other Goateenies?" asked Fred. "You know, Caruso, Gruff, and Bunny?"

"Well," said the captain, "I was hoping I might impose on you. I was hoping that they could stay here, rather permanently."

"Dad?" Noah asked hopefully.

Mr. Will put his hands in his pockets. "How much do you want for them?"

"Oh, nothing. Just a good home. I don't think they'll ever amount to much in a show."

"Dad?" asked Fred. "Please?"

"I'll have to talk this over with my wife. Meanwhile, would you like to let your other animals get out for some exercise?"

"Indeed, yes," said the captain. "They need fresh air."

"We were going to have a circus today," said Bailey. "But we don't have any good acts, except the elephant ballet, which we haven't even practiced."

Captain Calliope pushed a metal ramp up to the back of the truck and opened Finch's pen.

"Young lady, I think I might be of assistance. In exchange for some help with the original Great Goateenies this morning, they will perform for you this afternoon."

"Cool," Bailey said. She could see that Noah and Fred were pleased with the idea.

The captain handed her Finch's rope and she led him down the ramp. Finch was much larger than Gruff, and he was even harder to hold when he tugged. Fred grabbed Ruben's rope, and Noah tried to hang onto Bella's.

"These are strong goat dudes," Noah said.

"Ah, here comes my lovely Zola Mira," said Captain Calliope.

Bailey expected to see someone as old as the captain, maybe even like Sugar, arrive. She did not expect to see a slender, dark-haired woman get out of a new silver car and wave to all of them. She looked like a beauty queen.

"There you are. I found you," said Zola Mira.

"My lovely assistant," said Captain Calliope. "The act is nothing without her."

Zola Mira arched her thin eyebrows and flashed a smile that Bailey thought was phoney.

Captain Calliope turned to Mr. Will. "Please tell your wife that we'll be on the road after lunch. I'll collect my things, such as they are. We'll be able to catch up with the Otto Brothers in Emporia."

"What about the act?" asked Bailey. She was pulling Finch back toward the truck.

"You just wait," the captain said. "They don't call them the Great Goateenies for nothing."

43

Show Time

Aunt Coco drove up in her van shortly before noon. Sparrow waved wildly from the back porch. She wheeled her chair close to watch Aunt Coco's wheelchair lift work so she could get out of the van.

"I have a sandwich for you," said Sparrow. "I made it myself. And we're going to have a real circus, sort of."

"I'm ready," said her aunt. "I hope you have a tutu for me. These arms are ready to dance."

"Come in the house with me," Sparrow said.

"Sure enough," said Aunt Coco. "I've really worked up an appetite."

After making sure the original Great Goateenies had plenty of water where they were tied, Justin went home to get his little sisters so they could see the show.

Fred and Noah set up folding chairs near the barn door. They tried to tack sheets to the barn wall to make a tent, but they wouldn't stay up with broomstick poles.

"Sometimes things just don't work," said Noah.

"Aunt Coco says to close your eyes and imagine things," said Fred. "We'll just imagine the tent."

"Hah," said Noah. "Now for the props."

Bailey helped them remove the hoops, the folding platforms, stools, and the unicycle from the barn for the Goateenies' act.

"Do you think Gruff and Bunny feel bad that they're not in the show anymore?" she asked.

"Nah," said Noah. "Not if Mom lets them stay. They didn't like to do tricks. Especially Caruso."

"I guess we're ready," said Bailey. "Here comes Sugar with the popcorn."

Sugar parked her truck next to Aunt Coco's van and went in the house to greet her. When she came out, she set up her popcorn stand on a card table. "I haven't had this much fun in a long time. Popcorn. Get your popcorn!"

"I'll have some," said Fred.

"Well, Mr. Ringmaster, what's first—the Goateenies or the ballet?" Sugar asked.

"The ballet," Fred said.

"Then let's dress the pig," said Sugar with a laugh.

Bailey had never seen anything quite as ridiculous as Bunny wearing a tutu, unless it was Gruff or Goldie. Sugar's tutu was up under her armpits instead of around her waist.

Even though Fred and Noah had said they wouldn't participate, at the last minute they put on the tutus and did leaps through the yard to make Sparrow laugh.

"Not me," said Justin, sitting down with his sisters.

Goldie was pretty good about wearing hers, but Clover would have none of the little tutu collar Sugar made to go around her neck. She barked and tugged at it until it fell off, then ran off to bury it.

"We better do the parade quickly or the animals will all want to get rid of their costumes," said Sugar, turning on the polka music. "Now a big parade line, please. Sparrow wants to go first as Modoc."

"Just imagine fifty elephants," called out Aunt Coco. "Fifty lovely elephants all in a row. Now make elephant trunks with your arms, like this," she said.

"I can't do that and wheel my chair in the parade," said Sparrow.

"I'll push you," said Fred.

"Absurd," mumbled Zola Mira, leaning against the barn. "I've never seen anything so foolish in my life," as the little parade went by. She tapped her foot in annoyance.

"Join us," said Aunt Coco. "Use your imagination. It's lovely fun."

"Not just foolish, but ridiculous," said Zola Mira, crossing her arms. "In fact, this is the dumbest thing I've every seen. I thought this was going to be a quick stop. I want to get on the road."

Who cares what she thinks, thought Bailey.

44

The Great Goateenies

Zola Mira was still shaking her head when the elephant ballet ended four minutes later. "I think I got it all on tape," said Mr. Will. He turned off his camcorder.

"Take your seats, ladeez and gentlemen," said Fred. "The next act is Captain Cal-*eye*-o-pee and the Great Goateenies, assisted by Zola Mira."

"The lovely Zola Mira," whispered the captain, stroking his sideburns. "You didn't say name right."

"Oops, sorry. I forgot." Fred started over. "Presenting Captain *Cal*-ee-yoap, the *lovely* Zola Mira, and the Great Goateenies."

"Better," whispered the captain. "Now motion for everyone to clap. The Great Goateenies like applause."

"Put your hands together for the Great Goateenies," Fred shouted.

"And the lovely Zola Mira," whispered the captain. "She likes applause, too."

"Clap for the lovely Zola Mira!" Fred said loudly.

Zola Mira, wearing a glittery green, silver, and blue bodysuit stepped out of the barn and took a bow. She clapped her hands twice and out pranced Finch, Ruben, and Bella. The goats wore matching red harnesses with bells and cone-shaped hats with long white feathers.

Zola Mira pointed to an upside-down bucket. Bella walked over to it. "Let's see you count to five." Bella tapped her hoof on the bucket five times. "Now, tell us how many months there are in a year." Bella tapped the bucket twelve times.

"How does she know that?" Sparrow asked her aunt.

Aunt Coco just smiled.

Zola Mira continued. "How many stars are in the sky, Bella?"

Bella turned around and kicked the bucket.

"That's funny," said Justin's sister Fern.

"Finch, time to jump through the hoop," said Zola Mira. "I need a volunteer." She pointed to Bailey. She asked Bailey to hold one side of the hula hoop and she held the other. The goat backed up and charged at the hoop.

Bailey wanted to drop it, but held on tight and the goat sailed through.

"Ruben, I need a kiss," said Zola Mira, bending near the whiskery face. The goat kissed her.

"Peanut butter," whispered Sparrow to Aunt Coco.

"Now for the grand finale," said Captain Calliope. "The lovely Zola Mira will ask the Great Goateenies to do their world-famous pyramid while she rides the unicycle."

Zola Mira called each goat to come close to her. "Pyramid," she commanded

To Bailey's amazement, Finch dropped to the ground. Ruben crouched on his back, and Bella balanced on top. Zola Mira circled them three times on the unicycle with her hands high above her head.

"Ta-da," said Captain Calliope. He didn't need to wave his hands to ask for applause. Everyone clapped without prompting.

"That's all for today, folks. You'll just have to come see the full show," he said. "And now we must go. Otto Brothers, here we come."

Bleh, called Gruff from within the barn.

Bailey looked at the boys' mom.

"Yes, they can stay," said Miss Bekka. "Keswick Inn needs its own Goateenies."

45

Starting Over

"I really enjoyed myself today," said Sugar. "Sparrow and Aunt Coco seemed to have a particularly good time in the ballet." She set the box of tutus on the small porch table.

"Zola Mira thought it was stupid," said Bailey. "She is pretty stuck up."

"You can't please everyone," said Sugar. "It was just fun to be positively silly for a few minutes." Sugar kicked off her old sneakers. "I don't know about you, but the popcorn has worn off, and I'm ready to grill something for supper—maybe burgers and garden vegetables."

"Yum," said Bailey. She eased into her purple rocker and closed her eyes. Sugar opened the screen door to let the cats out to join them and then sat back in her rocker.

"Shall we try your mother tonight?" Sugar asked. "We might get a better connection."

"I don't know," said Bailey. She put her feet on the railing.

"I've got to confess. I heard part of your conversation with Molly," said Sugar.

"All she wanted to talk about was her dumb dress," said Bailey.

"She's excited about the wedding," said Sugar. "But what I wanted to say was that I was proud of you."

Bailey turned quickly to look at her grandmother's face. "You were?"

"Yes, you politely told her how you felt about her getting married."

"Didn't matter," said Bailey, looking away again.

"Of course it does," said Sugar, resting her feet next to Bailey's on the porch rail. "You can't control what she does or says, but you let her know what's on your mind, and that counts for a lot. It's like letting a caged bird from inside you go free."

Bailey leaned back in her chair. She realized that she did feel a little better.

"Now, would you like to go to the mall tomorrow afternoon to look for new curtains?" asked her grandmother.

"Sure." Bailey thought for a moment. "Maybe Emily could come with us."

"Good idea," said Sugar. Her face crinkled into a warm smile. "That's my wonderful Wild Woman."

Discussion Questions

1. Captain Calliope's arrival at Keswick Inn gets Bailey thinking about visiting the circus when she lived in Florida. She was thinking it would be fun to be part of the circus. Would you want to be in a circus? What job would you want to have? Give three reasons why you would or would not want to join a circus.

2. Bailey doubts Captain Calliope's ability to train the animals as he plans. Do you think he is a loser? A dreamer? Why or why not?

3. Why do you think Zola Mira and the other Goateenies left the act? Write the conversation Zola Mira had with Captain Calliope when they parted ways. Do you think they were ever that great? Is "great" the same as "famous"? Why or why not?

4. Sparrow is a foster child and now it seems an aunt she never met might want to claim

her. Who do you think is Sparrow's family? What is a family anyway?

5. How does Bailey first react to the news that her mother may marry Dr. Snorge-Swinson?

6. At Emily's slumber party, Sierra makes fun of the kids' circus as "juvenile." She steps on Bailey's hot dog and spills her drink. How does the author show you rather than tell you that Sierra is mean? What else does she say or do?

7. Have you ever been in a situation where you saw or experienced bullying? How did you feel? Were you tempted to join in the bullying? Did you want to run away like Emily? Why do you think people join in or run away when there is bullying?

8. Bullying seems to go on between kids all too much. At what point should you tell an adult about bullying behavior you have experienced or observed? What if the adults say, "Oh, that is just the way kids behave—" and you don't agree? What if the adults overreact?

9. Feeling safe and respected is very important to every human being. What can you do if you are not feeling safe and respected? What did Bailey do when Sierra was so mean at the slumber party?

10. During and after the very bad thunderstorm, Miss Bekka calls Sugar and Bailey on her cell phone to check on them. Having good neighbors can be really important. What kind of neighbors do you have? Do you sometimes check on each other?

11. Plan a backyard circus, puppet show, or concert. Invite friends and family of every age to participate. Make tickets, programs, and costumes.

12. Would you say Bailey is jealous, disappointed, or angry about her mother's engagement to Dr. Andrew Snorge-Swinsen? What happened on the Webcam and in the e-mails to convince Bailey that she is losing her mother and not gaining a father? Has she misinterpreted her mother's behavior?

13. What if Aunt Coco had turned out to be the villain the children feared? Write the scene of a completely different Aunt Coco who has come to take Sparrow away.

14. What if Captain Calliope had not found Zola Mira and the real Goateenies? Pretend Miss Bekka gets a phone call from the police. Captain Calliope needs the Keswicks' help because . . .

Web Sites

Circus

http://circusworld.wisconsinhistory.org/

http://www.circusinamerica.org/public/

http://www.barbwired.com/barbweb/programs/
stravinsky_polka.html

http://www.elephants.com/index.php

http://www.beattycircus.com/

http://www.ringling.com/

http://www.Ringling.org/

www.Bigapplecircus.org/

www.gotothecircus.com

http://en.wikipedia.org/wiki/
Bailey%27s_Crossroads,_Virginia

Goats and Pigs

http://www.goatworld.com/articles/goatslife/
goatfacts.shtml

http://www.workinggoats.com/?id=75

http://www.potbellypigpets.com/
characteristics.html

http://www.valentinesperformingpigs.com/

Loggerhead Sea Turtles

http://kids.nationalgeographic.com/Animals/
CreatureFeature/Loggerhead

http://animaldiversity.ummz.umich.edu/site/
accounts/information/Caretta_caretta.html

Luray Caverns

http://www.luraycaverns.com/

(Web sites were available at press time. Author
and publisher have no control over their content or
links to other Web sites.)

From Sugar's Bookshelves

Ballet of the Elephants, Leda Schubert
Born on the Circus, Fred Powledge
Charlotte's Web, E. B. White
Mystery of the Circus Clown, The, Adler, David A. Adler
Step Right Up! The Adventure of Circus in America, LaVahn G. Hoh, and William H. Rough
Toby Tyler: Or Ten Weeks with a Circus, James Otis
Traveling Showmen: The American Circus Before The Civil War, Stuart Thayer
When the Circus Came to Town, Laurence Yep

And, listen to the "Circus Polka" by Igor Stravinksy. Sugar's CD is by the Dresden Philharmonic Orchestra, Herbert Kegel, conductor

Glossary

butt: hit with horns or head.

calliope: a musical instrument that makes whistle sounds by using steam.

chaff: seed and debris from straw or grain.

dormer: a window projected from a sloping roof.

iguana: a large lizard that eats mostly vegetation.

menagerie: a collection of various animals.

nubby: knobby, like small bumpy horns.

pride: a group of lions.

scrounge: steal or swipe.

spangling: sparkling; glittering.

tarp / tarpaulin: strong, often waterproof material made with tar to protect buildings.

Goats, roosters and hens live on the Andersons' farm near Lake Anna, Virginia. Bailey and Sugar like to visit the farm and buy fresh brown eggs there.

The Andersons' goats have a playhouse. They like to climb into it and look around at the pigs and chickens. Even the female goats have horns.

The Andersons also have potbellied pigs. These pigs are old and like to sleep a lot. The Andersons are careful to give them only good food (and just a little) so that the pigs don't become overweight—even for pigs.

Loggerhead Sea Turtles

Loggerhead turtles are a "threatened" species for many reasons. Early in our history, turtles were prized as food and were hunted heavily.

Now, animals, such as raccoons, invade their nests and people have built houses along the beaches. The lights from the houses confuse the hatching babies. The young turtles normally are attracted to the brighter sky over the water and crawl to the water when they hatch. However, if there are bright lights, instead of heading for the ocean or Gulf, the hatchlings crawl toward land where they can't survive once the sun comes up. During nesting season, everyone is must have "lights out for turtles." Turtles may also become tangled in fishing nets and drown, or be injured by boat propellers.

Females may lay a "clutch" of 100 to 126 round eggs at a time. It takes fifty-five to sixty days for the eggs to incubate and hatch in Florida. Most of the hatchlings do not survive, even if they make it to the sea as they are favorite food of many marine animals.

Many of the barrier islands on the coast have groups of volunteers called "the turtle patrol." These folks go out very early each morning during the nesting season (May and June) and look for fresh nests, which they record and mark so beachgoers won't disturb them. Then they go out again in the fall to record which nests have hatched.

One night Bailey and her mother watched a loggerhead turtle laying her eggs in a nest she dug in the sand on Sanibel Island. You can see the turtle's tracks (arrows) where her flippers pushed the sand away as she climbed the dune.

Adult loggerhead turtles can grow to be almost three feet long and may weigh as much as 200 pounds. They may live more than thirty years. They travel hundreds or even thousands of miles each year before they return to the same beaches where they were hatched to lay their eggs.

The next morning, the turtle patrol marked the new nest with yellow tape and signs to protect it.

An actual photograph of the the ballet of the elephants in Madison Square Garden, New York City. Courtesy of the Circus World Museum, Baraboo, Wisconsin.

Acknowledgments

I am grateful for wonderful assistance, suggestions, and advice provided by many people, including: My husband, Jim Salisbury; Nancy Miller for her discussion questions; Abbie Grotke, Elizabeth Madden, David Black, Julie Franklin, Dr. Lenn Johns; Bert and Barbara Stafford; Brenda Anderson of Anderson Farms; Hallie Vaughan, Emily Searle, and Scotty Register.

And a special thanks to author and circus expert LaVahn Hoh, professor of drama at the University of Virginia.

About the Author

 Linda Salisbury draws her inspiration for the Bailey Fish Adventure series from her experiences in Florida and Virginia, and as a mother, grandmother, mentor, and foster mother. She is a musician and enjoys boating and traveling.

Also in the Bailey Fish Adventure series are: *The Wild Women of Lake Anna,* a *ForeWord* magazine finalist for Book of the Year 2005; *No Sisters Sisters Club,* silver finalist in Florida Publishers Association's Best Children's Fiction 2008; *The Thief at Keswick Inn* (winner of the FPA, President's Pick Award 2007); *The Mysterious Jamestown Suitcase* (a bronze medalist in the Moonbeam Children's Book Awards and *ForeWord* finalist); *Ghost of the Chicken Coop Theater;* and *Trouble in Contrary Woods.* She's also the author of *Mudd*

Saves the Earth: Booger Glue, Cow Diapers and Other G̶o̶o̶d̶ Ideas.

About the Illustrator

 Illustrator and book designer Carol Tornatore lives in Nokomis, Florida, with her Siamese cats. She has won numerous awards for her innovative book and magazine designs. Some of her other children's books include *Florida A to Z, The Runaway Bed, Zachary Cooks Up Some Fun*, and the *Southern Fossil Discovery* series. She enjoys going to the beach, collecting sea shells, and dancing.